DOCTOR WHO
PLANET OF GIANTS

DOCTOR WHO
PLANET OF GIANTS

based on the BBC television series by Louis Marks by arrangement with BBC Books, a division of BBC Enterprises Ltd

TERRANCE DICKS

Number 145 in the
Target Doctor Who Library

A TARGET BOOK
published by
the Paperback Division of
W H Allen & Co Plc

A Target Book
Published in 1990
By the Paperback Division of
W H Allen & Co Plc
Sekforde House, 175/9 St John Street, London EC1V 4LL

The BBC producer was Verity Lambert
The directors were Mervyn Pinfield and Douglas Camfield
The role of the Doctor was played by William Hartnell

Printed and bound in Great Britain by
Cox & Wyman Ltd, Reading, Berkshire

ISBN 0 426 20345 3

Contents

1

Dangerous Landfall

It was a beautiful summer's day. From a clear blue sky, the sun shone down on the perfect country cottage, in the perfect English country garden.

The cottage had a thatched roof, green lawns, blossoming flower beds, a thriving vegetable patch and a stone-flagged patio. It was a place to dream of: the ideal weekend retreat, a long-awaited haven for retirement.

It was also the home of an unseen menace that threatened all life on Earth. Soon, it was to be the scene of the Doctor's most grotesque and terrifying adventure.

'We're approaching a planet now,' announced the Doctor. Inside the extraordinary space-time vessel called the TARDIS, a tense little group gathered around the many-sided central control console. At first sight, they formed a strange, ill-assorted company.

Busy at the controls was the Doctor himself, a white-haired old man with a lined and wrinkled face, an aristocratic beak of a nose, and eyes that blazed with a fierce intelligence. He wore an antiquated-looking frock-coat, a cravat and a high-winged collar, check trousers and old-fashioned boots, the whole ensemble topped with a furcollared cloak.

Beside him stood a slim dark-haired young woman in slacks and a crisp white blouse, her face set in her habitual expression of mild disapproval. Her name was Barbara Wright and no child would have been very surprised to learn that she was, or rather had been, a school teacher.

Next to her was a cheerful-looking young man in sports jacket and flannels, complete with collar and tie and a handkerchief in the top pocket. He too was a teacher and his name was Ian Chesterton.

The fourth member of the group was the youngest, a girl of about sixteen wearing denim dungarees. She had short dark hair and big dark eyes. Her name was Susan Foreman and she called the Doctor 'grandfather'.

It was Susan who was responsible for the presence of Ian and Barbara in the TARDIS. During her brief spell as a pupil at Coal Hill School in the London of the 1960s, the extraordinary range of Susan's knowledge – and the even stranger gaps in it – had aroused their curiosity to such an extent that they had followed her home.

To their astonishment they had discovered that home was a police box in a junkyard and that the grandfather with whom Susan claimed to live was the amazing old man known only as the Doctor. With the best of intentions, Ian and Barbara had forced their way into the TARDIS and had promptly been carried off through space and time to an extraordinary series of adventures. Ricocheting between Earth and a variety of alien planets they had encountered cave men, Daleks, the warriors of Kublai Khan, the Voords of Marinus, a murderous Aztec priest, and the extraordinary dome-headed Sensorites.

In many ways, their most recent adventure had been the most unsettling of all. Once again the Doctor had managed to get them back to Earth, and once again he had landed them in quite the wrong time-period, and in deadly danger. Instead of the London of the swinging Sixties they had found themselves confronted with the Paris of the French Revolution, where they had come perilously near to losing their heads. They had become embroiled with the plots of an English secret agent called James Stirling, and had witnessed the bloody downfall of the tyrant Robespierre, at the hands of the Revolution he had done so much to bring about.

Somehow the fact that this terrifying adventure was taking place on Earth made things seem worse, rather than better. It bore out one of the

Doctor's favourite sayings: that of all the savage species in the galaxy, few were more dangerous and bloodthirsty than man . . .

Now they were about to try again.

It was Ian who reacted to the Doctor's announcement that they were approaching a planet. With an expression of cheerful scepticism he asked: 'Which one?' His tone indicated that he didn't expect the Doctor to have the answer.

The Doctor shot Ian an offended glance. Despite frequent demonstrations of his inability to steer the TARDIS with any real accuracy, he bitterly resented any allusion to the problem. With an air of infuriating smugness he said: 'Well, we shall soon see!'

You would never believe, thought Ian to himself, that so far the old boy had got it wrong every single time.

As a matter of fact, the Doctor was feeling pretty confident. The fact that on his last landing he had once again managed to reach the right planet was a considerable help. It left only the time co-ordinates to be sorted out. This time the Doctor was pretty sure he had pulled it off. All the instrument-readings bore him out. They were on Earth, in England, and the year was 1963. Susan and he would soon be free of their irritating companions and able to resume their travels. What could possibly go wrong?

The Doctor was about to find out.

It started innocently enough: Barbara rested

her hand idly on the console, then snatched it away. 'Ouch!'

The Doctor looked up from the controls. 'What's the matter?'

'It's hot – I nearly burned myself.'

'Hot? Where?'

The Doctor touched the part of the console that Barbara indicated, and gave a sharp intake of breath. 'Yes, some overheating going on there, I'm afraid. It's just as well we're landing. Susan, check the fault indicator please.'

As Susan ran to an instrument panel built into the TARDIS wall, Barbara regarded the central console with alarm, 'It won't blow up, will it?'

'No, of course not,' said the Doctor huffily. But he looked worried all the same. 'It's just that . . . well, there we were in France in the middle of the eighteenth century . . .' His voice tailed off and he looked vague for a moment, as if the complexity of it all was getting beyond even him.

Barbara gave him a worried look, and the Doctor rallied. 'I've tried a new navigational sequence to side-step the ship to England in the middle of the twentieth century.'

You mean you've taken a wild stab at it in the vague hope that this time it will work out all right, thought Barbara to herself. But she didn't say it out loud. The Doctor would only have denied it indignantly, and told her she was too ignorant to understand.

Susan was studying the instrument panel.

'There's a reading on QR18, grandfather, and another on A14D. Both are on yellow standby.'

The Doctor studied the control console. The rise of the centre column was slowing perceptibly now. 'Another minute and we'll be landing . . .'

'Those fault indicator readings,' began Ian.

'What? Oh, QR18 concerns the atmospheric pressure outside the ship, and AD14 is the ship's weight.'

'And the yellow stand-by?'

'A yellow stand-by warns us to examine the two at the earliest opportunity.' The Doctor stared abstractedly into space. 'Hmm, pressure and weight . . .'

Suddenly an alarm signal blared out.

'Grandfather, the doors,' shouted Susan. She pointed. 'Something's wrong with the doors!'

They all turned and saw that the TARDIS doors were beginning to open.

The Doctor sprang to the console, and threw a switch. Nothing happened. 'Close them, Chesterton,' he shouted. 'We haven't fully materialized yet. *Close them*!'

Ian ran to the door and hurled himself against them. They seemed quite immovable and he felt all the helplessness of man against machine. Barbara and Susan came to help him: all three heaved frantically, and suddenly the doors gave way to their joint efforts and closed.

Gasping, Ian turned round and saw that the Doctor was leaning on the console, one hand supporting him, the other clasped to his forehead.

Ian went over to him. 'Are you all right, Doctor?' The Doctor didn't reply and Ian touched him gently on the shoulder.

The Doctor started. 'Eh? What is it?'

'Are you all right? I thought you seemed . . .'

'Don't bother me now,' snapped the Doctor and returned to his brooding.

Barbara came over to them. 'What happened just then?'

Ignoring her, the Doctor turned to Susan. 'Susan, get back to the fault indicator. I want everything checked – *everything*, do you hear?'

'Yes, grandfather.' Susan hurried away.

Barbara tried to make the best of things. 'Well, nothing very much seems to have happened to us . . .'

The Doctor whirled round, eyes blazing with anger. 'Don't be childish! They opened. The doors opened before we had properly landed.'

Ian did his best top keep the peace. 'We realize what happened, Doctor, but what does it mean? You don't have to hide things from us.'

'That's right,' said Barbara encouragingly. 'Don't keep us in suspense.'

Her well-meaning cheerfulness provoked yet another of the Doctor's explosions. 'Stop bothering me with your futile questions! Can't you see?'

Ian was beginning to get angry. 'No, we can't see, Doctor. That's just the trouble.'

'We were at the point of materializing, entering the time of a planet as well as its space, and the doors opened *before* we'd properly adjusted.'

Barbara was struggling to understand. 'You mean something might have gone out of the ship, through those doors?'

The Doctor shook his head decisively. 'No, that isn't possible.'

'Something came inside?' suggested Ian.

'You are both thinking on an everyday level.' said the Doctor scornfully. 'This isn't one of your supersonic aircraft: I am talking about time travel. Look, it's simple enough to move a chair from room to room in a house, eh? But to move that chair from a house in 1796 to a house in 1964 is a different matter altogether.' He looked at their blank faces and said exasperatedly: 'I see you have no idea what I'm talking about.'

'You've never explained the method by which the TARDIS travels,' said Ian acidly. 'How could we?'

Susan came back from her study of the fault indicator. 'Everything seems to be all right, now, grandfather,' she said in a puzzled voice. 'There isn't a fault shown anywhere, not even any yellow stand-bys.'

The Doctor didn't seem to be particularly reassured. 'But something must have happened . . . I'll check the fault indicator myself, just to be sure.' He glared reprovingly at Ian. 'You see, you wouldn't attempt to swim underwater with your mouth open, would you? Does that make things any clearer to you?' And with that he marched over to the fault indicator.

Barbara sighed. 'I wish he wouldn't talk in riddles like that.'

Ian turned to Susan. 'Perhaps you can help us.'

'I know that the trickiest time of all is the moment of materialization. It's a question of displacement.' Susan frowned, trying to make them understand. 'If you put a dish in a bowl of water, the water rises, doesn't it?'

'Yes of course, that's simple,' said Barbara impatiently.

'But, suppose the water was filling the bowl to the very top and there was a tight lid on as well? There'd be no room for displacement. Well, it's rather like that when the weight of the TARDIS suddenly enters the atmosphere. Something has to give way.'

Ian shrugged. 'The air, presumably . . .'

The Doctor spoke without looking up from the fault indicator. 'Exactly! And the atmospheric pressure on Earth is fourteen point seven pounds to the square inch. You're getting the idea, Chesterton. It's all right when the TARDIS is fully materialized, the envelope of air can always give way somewhere.'

'Just as we're entering the time dimension,' said Susan. 'That's the danger point.'

The Doctor turned away from the fault indicator. 'Still, there doesn't seem to be any harm done.' He came over to Barbara. 'Was I rude to you just now, Barbara? If so, I'm sorry. I'm afraid I tend to forget the niceties when I'm under pressure. Do forgive me.'

Barbara smiled, almost in spite of herself. 'That's all right, Doctor. There's nothing to forgive.'

The Doctor touched her gently on the shoulder and went back to the control console. 'I hope none of you realized just how worried I was. There is nothing worse than the horror of the unknown.' He frowned down at the console. 'I suppose everything's all right. And yet . . .' He shook his head, studying the instrument readings. 'Well, it's safe to go outside anyway. Air, temperature, all as they should be. Turn on the scanner, Susan, and let's have a look at where we are.'

Susan switched on the scanner, but all it produced was a blur of static.

'Perhaps it needs a new tube,' suggested Ian.

The Doctor gave him a withering look. 'This isn't one of your primitive Earth television sets, Chesterton.'

'Well, we must look outside for ourselves,' said Barbara brightly. 'You said it was safe, Doctor.'

She glanced at Ian and felt sure that they were sharing the same thoughts. Had it worked this time? Were they really home, back in their own time and place?

'Go outside,' said the Doctor vaguely. 'Yes, though I still wonder why . . . Well, we shall just have to go and see.'

'Shall I open the door, grandfather?' asked Susan.

The Doctor nodded, and she operated the door control.

The doors opened smoothly, and everyone moved towards them.

'Cautiously now, all of you,' warned the Doctor.

They went out to face what the Doctor himself had called 'the horror of the unknown'.

2

The Unknown

Susan and Barbara went out first, and as the Doctor moved to follow them, Ian asked: 'What forced the doors open then, Doctor?'

'The pressure of the atmosphere into which we were materializing, my boy, multiplied some sixty or seventy times.' The Doctor glanced back around the brightly lit TARDIS control-room, which was humming quietly with energy and apparently very much its normal self. 'Yet we seem to have come out of it unscathed. At the moment it's a complete mystery to me . . .'

'We seem to be in a mountain pass, or something,' called Barbara from outside the door.

Ian and the Doctor hurried outside, and the Doctor closed the TARDIS doors behind them.

They found Susan and Barbara staring up at

the walls of a kind of canyon. The Doctor scanned the high rock walls stretching away to left and right. They were broken up on either side and in both directions, by junction points with other canyons, leading in turn, the Doctor guessed, to yet more canyons. It was as though they were standing in a giant maze.

'Now, why wouldn't the scanner show us this?' he demanded indignantly.

'Perhaps that was the only damage the ship suffered,' suggested Ian. 'Some kind of overloading on the scanner circuits.'

'I suppose it's possible,' admitted the Doctor grumpily. He preferred his own solutions to those offered by others. He peered at the canyon wall. 'Strange sort of rock formation, Chesterton.'

'Yes, it is, isn't it?' said Ian thoughtfully.

Barbara came to join them. A born teacher, she was always eager to impart useful information. 'There are two different kinds of rock, have you noticed? This top part is stone, but the underneath part is quite different.'

'Very observant, my dear,' said the Doctor drily. 'And what's this, Chesterton? Look here. Is it concrete?

Ian bent down and looked where the Doctor was pointing. 'Might be.'

'But a very rough kind, surely,' mused the Doctor.

Ian nodded thoughtfully. 'Yes, it is. Maybe it's a new kind – sort of pebbles of sand . . .'

'Something manufactured, anyway,' said the

Doctor. 'Made to keep this great stone in place, to fix it firmly to the ground beneath . . .'

Susan looked puzzled. 'I would have thought this rock was big enough to stay where it was anyway, without sticking it down.'

'Yes, all very odd,' muttered the Doctor. He rose and looked around him. They seemed to be at some sort of junction, with canyons straggling away both to left and right.

'Well now,' said the Doctor briskly. 'Obviously, we must explore. I suggest that Barbara and I explore this pass to the left, Chesterton, while you and Susan go to the right.'

Ian Chesterton sighed. This was the Doctor at his most aggravating, he thought: taking charge, giving orders, and sending himself and everyone else straight into danger. He looked hard at the Doctor, and the Doctor looked back defiantly, eyes alight with mischievous challenge. 'All right,' said Ian resignedly. 'But stay within calling distance. Sing out if you find anything, and we'll do the same.'

'Yes, yes, yes,' said the Doctor and bustled Barbara away. As always, he was eager to discover the secrets of their new and strange environment.

They moved along the left-hand branch of the canyon, the Doctor peering at the walls and muttering to himself while Barbara looked ahead. It was Barbara who saw the strange object draped across the wall of the canyon just in front of them.

'Look, Doctor, what's that tube thing?'

She moved a little closer, and then drew back with a gasp of horror. 'It seems to be some sort of huge snake. Shall we call the others?'

The Doctor was childishly reluctant to share their discovery. 'No, not yet . . .' He cautiously approached the huge snake-like form. 'I think, yes, I think it's dead.'

Barbara was relieved. 'It's a fantastic size . . .'

The Doctor peered thoughtfully up at the monstrous shape. 'No eyes, no distinct head as such.' He reached up and prodded the thing. 'Hmm, the skin is interesting.'

Barbara shuddered. 'Interesting?'

'Yes . . . quite dull, you see?'

Barbara was struck by an unwelcome thought. 'Are you sure it isn't just sleeping?'

'No, no, it's dead all right,' said the Doctor positively. 'Death has it's own particular posture and appearance, my dear. Shall we go on?'

As they moved away, the Doctor said thoughtfully: 'The point that has to concern us, you see, is what killed that creature? The thing was massive, so whatever killed it is presumably even bigger and stronger.'

'Perhaps it died naturally,' suggested Barbara hopefully.

'No, no, the thing, whatever it was, died suddenly and violently. Murder has its own posture and appearance too . . .'

Exploring their branch of the enormous maze,

Ian and Susan were just about to come across something equally mysterious and worrying.

Ian moved his forehead. 'That sun's really blazing down, isn't it?'

Susan didn't reply. She was looking down at a strange object in the path ahead. 'Hey, look what I've found!' She knelt down to examine it. It was white, or rather off-white, and about the same size and shape as a football.

Ian bent down beside her. 'Odd looking thing . . . It's not an egg, is it? No, it can't be, not at this size,' He prodded the round object: it felt tough and leathery. 'Ostriches? Surely their eggs are more oval than this . . .'

He heard Susan's voice from further down the path. 'There's a whole pile of them over here . . .' Suddenly her voice rose higher. '*Ian*!'

The fear in her voice brought Ian running to her side. He found Susan at another of the innumerable junctions, staring upward in horror.

Ian looked up too. Looming over them both, glaring down malevolently from the edge of the canyon, was the terrifying form of a giant ant.

3

The Terrible Truth

Taking Susan's arm, Ian tried to pull her away, but she resisted. 'It's all right, Ian. I'm pretty sure it's dead.'

Ian stared upwards at the motionless insect. 'Yes, you're right. Just look at the size of it – the thing must be two or three feet long!'

Susan pointed to another of the grey-white spheres, clasped between the dead ant's front legs. 'It looks as if it was trying to carry that egg.'

The science teacher in Ian reasserted itself. Like Barbara, he could never resist imparting useful information. 'That's a normal reaction for an ant. When a nest is being attacked, for instance, it will carry the eggs to safety: a worker ant will give its life rather than abandon them.'

'It looks as if the ant couldn't have had much

of a chance,' said Susan. 'When it was attacked, I mean. It must have died very quickly.'

Ian nodded. 'Yes, and there are all these other eggs just left lying about. That's just not normal. Either the other ants were frightened away, or they're all dead too.'

Susan studied the ant's contorted body. 'This one looks as if it died in agony. Look at the way its legs are all twisted up.'

Ian didn't reply. He stood staring up at the huge dead insect in horrified fascination.

'What are you thinking?' asked Susan.

Ian shuddered. 'I was just wondering . . . what sort of world would be able to produce an insect that size?'

'Look Doctor,' called Barbara. 'There's another of those giant snake things.'

The Doctor came to join her, and stood studying the segmented snake-like body that dangled over the canyon edge. Suddenly he chuckled. 'This isn't another of the creatures, Barbara. It's the other end of the one we saw earlier – *both* ends must be dangling over the edge. The thing must be enormous . . . I'm pretty sure I know what it is now. I recognize the species. It's an earthworm: a giant earthworm!'

'Not from my Earth,' said Barbara definitely.

The Doctor frowned. 'There are places on your Earth that I've never visited, such as Africa and Australasia. Isn't it possible there are worms the size of this one in some remote part of your planet?'

'No, I'm positive there aren't,' said Barbara. 'Not of a really incredible size like that.'

'Mmm . . .' The Doctor rubbed his chin. 'Yet the resemblance is so close. Except for the size, I'd be prepared to swear it is from your planet.'

Shaking her head, Barbara looked around. The opening of several more junctions could be seen. 'It's a bit like a maze, isn't it? We mustn't get lost.'

'We won't,' said the Doctor confidently. 'But I'm determined not to go back without reaching some definite conclusions. All we have so far is a phenomenon . . .' he gestured towards the giant worm, 'a phenomenon and a mystery.'

'What mystery?'

'This maze, as you call it. It appears to be haphazard, yet it seems to me there's a kind of pattern to it. And a pattern suggests a brain at work – a brain with some kind of purpose. Come along, let's keep going!'

Tireless as ever when his scientific curiosity was aroused, the Doctor set off at a brisk pace. Wearily, Barbara trailed after him.

Meanwhile, Ian and Susan were continuing their journey through the seemingly endless maze of stone canyons. They'd agreed to check one side of the canyon each, Susan the left and Ian the right.

'I've counted at least six of those dead ants, Ian,' said Susan after a while.

'Yes,' said Ian thoughtfully. 'I've seen quite a few on this side too.'

They turned a corner – and stopped in their tracks. Facing them was an enormous picture of a flower – a sort of giant poster, mounted on a wooden stake that seemed almost as big as a telegraph pole.

Ian peered up at it. 'What on Earth . . .'

'It looks like a picture of night-scented stock,' said Susan helpfully.

'So it does, but why would anyone put up a picture of it here?'

For a moment, Ian thought the thing must be an advertising poster. But the massive stake was not fastened properly: it was just jammed through a hole in the paper square. And why would anyone put up a poster in a place like this? 'I just don't get it,' he muttered.

Susan read out the words printed in giant letters beneath the flower picture. 'Ralph Seed Company Limited, Norwich.' She looked excitedly up at Ian. 'Norwich is in England, isn't it? In Norfolk.'

'That's right. We're on Earth, and we're in England. But where, precisely, are we? Why this maze of rock canyons? Why the giant ants . . . and now this thing?' Ian was struck by a sudden inspiration. 'Perhaps it's some kind of crazy advertising exhibition – you know, giant-sized models and all that. I'm going to take a look round the other side.'

Meanwhile, Barbara and the Doctor had made a strange discovery of their own. It was less spectacular than Ian and Susan's, but to the Doctor, at least, it was just as significant.

Barbara noticed a sort of long white pole, leaning against the side of the canyon. She reached out and touched it, and the pole toppled to the ground, narrowly missing her head.

The Doctor, who could move amazingly quickly in an emergency, yanked her out of harm's way.

'Are you all right, my dear? That could have given you a very nasty headache!'

Before the shaken Barbara could reply, the Doctor was on his knees examining the fallen pole. 'Now this is interesting. This piece of wood had obviously been cut with machinery . . .'

Barbara couldn't see the reason for the Doctor's evident excitement. 'I thought it was just a length of timber. I mean, that's what it is, isn't it?'

The Doctor stood up, pointing to the other end of the square-cut pole, which was blackened and charred by fire. 'Surely you know what this is, Barbara. It is quite clearly a matchstick.'

Barbara smiled. 'Well, yes, I suppose it does look like one.'

'It doesn't just look like one,' said the Doctor sharply. 'It *is* a matchstick!'

'But it can't be, not at that size . . .'

'My dear Barbara, can't you see? First that gigantic earthworm, and now this! Don't you understand what's happened to us?'

Perhaps because her mind was more open to the unusual, not to say the fantastic, Susan was coming to the same conclusion as the Doctor.

Ian, however, was still blissfully unaware of the true state of affairs. On the other side of the strange flower poster they had found what Susan took as a confirmation of her growing fears. Ian, however, interpreted their find quite differently.

'How's this for advertising, Susan?' He looked admiringly up at the giant half-open matchbox before them. 'This must be some kind of special advertising exhibition, like the World's Fair or something. We've landed right in the middle of it!

'No, Ian,' said Susan quietly.'

'What else could it be? Look at the scale of this thing!'

Ian clambered on top of the half-open matchbox and sat down, dangling his legs inside. 'All I'm wondering is exactly what part of the world we're in. An exhibition like this could be anywhere – London, Paris, New York . . .' He spoke with a note of strain in his voice, like a man obstinately refusing to face the facts.

'You're wrong, Ian,' said Susan. 'Completely wrong. I started to realize what must have happened when I saw that seed packet.'

'All right then, what's your theory?'

'All these things we've been seeing: they haven't been made bigger,' said Susan calmly, '*we've* been made smaller. Ian, we've been reduced in size – we're only one inch high!'

4

The Destroyer

Not far away, the Doctor was breaking the same astonishing news. 'Yes, Barbara, I'd say we've been reduced to a size of about one inch. You, me – all of us, the TARDIS as well. We must find the others at once and get back to the ship.'

Too astonished even to argue, Barbara followed him.

Ian, however, was still arguing vigorously. 'No Susan, you can't be right. You just can't.'

'I am – I know I am,' insisted Susan. 'This is what grandfather was half afraid of when the ship doors opened while we were landing. He simply wouldn't admit it was possible, that's all.'

'But it isn't possible,' protested Ian. 'It's ridiculous!'

'Oh, Ian, work it out for yourself. When the doors were open, outside pressure forced us to reduce in size to survive.'

Before Ian could reply a shadow fell over them, a shadow so huge that it seemed to darken the sky. A terrible rumbling, crunching sound filled the air.

'What is it?' shouted Susan.

From on top of the matchbox, Ian yelled: 'Run Susan. Run!' He tried to jump down, but the open matchbox seemed to shudder and he tumbled helplessly inside.

Terrified, Susan dashed to the side of the canyon and huddled into a niche in the rock walls.

A plump, grey-suited man walked along the stone-flagged path towards the cottage. He wore a black Homburg hat and carried an official-looking briefcase. Spotting a matchbox on the path he bent down, puffing a little, and picked it up.

Farrow was a civil servant. 'Waste not, want not' had always been his favourite motto.

The crunching sound moved away, the shadow lifted and Susan emerged from her hiding place. She began running blindly the way they had come, turned a corner, and ran straight into the Doctor and Barbara.

She stared wildly at them, gasping for breath.

Barbara looked at her in alarm. 'Susan, what's the matter?'

'It's Ian . . .'

'What about Ian?' snapped the Doctor. 'What's happened to him?'

Susan's story came out in a breathless rush. 'We found a matchbox, a huge one . . . Ian climbed on to it. Then it went dark and there was this terrible noise . . . I saw Ian fall into the matchbox, right inside it. I ran and hid, and when I came out the matchbox had gone!'

Barbara put and arm round Susan's shoulders. 'All right, all right . . .'

'Well, it's quite clear what's happened,' said the Doctor, logical as always. 'Someone must have come along and picked the matchbox up!'

Ian could have confirmed the Doctor's theory, though at the moment he was in no position to do so. He was shut up in a confined space, being jolted to and fro in total darkness, trying to dodge a collection of long wooden poles rattling about in the blackness with him. One of them hit him on the shoulder, giving him a nasty bruise.

Ian was inside the matchbox, being carried along in Farrow's hand . . .

Farrow followed the crazy-paving of the path to the wide stone-flagged patio outside the house and sank gratefully down on a garden chair.

He put his briefcase on the ground beside him,

arranged cigarettes and matches close by, and sat back mopping his brow.

The Doctor and his companions had made their way to a point where both walls of the canyon were low and irregular enough to be climbed.

Susan started to scramble up, but the Doctor pushed her aside. 'No, no, my dear, let me . . .'

With much huffing and groaning, and with a lot of help from Barbara and Susan, the Doctor managed to get high enough to peer over the edge. He studied the scene before him, pleased to have his theory confirmed.

Stretching directly ahead was a huge stone plain broken up by a network of cracks. This, of course, was simply the crazy-paving of the path that led up to the house. The maze of canyons in which they had been wandering was formed by the gaps between the irregularly-shaped flagstones of the path.

Far in the distance the Doctor could see the cottage, and the man sitting on the patio.

Susan called from below. 'Can you see anything, Doctor?'

'There's a house up here in the distance – and a man sitting down. The distances seem tremendous. Get me down now, will you?'

Getting the Doctor down safely seemed almost harder than getting him up, but they managed it in the end.

'This man you saw,' asked Barbara. 'Was he the one who took the matchbox?'

The Doctor shrugged. 'How on Earth do I know?'

'I know you don't *know*, but it's possible, isn't it?'

'I suppose so.'

He sounded infuriatingly vague and Barbara snapped: 'You could at least give us some hope, Doctor. How far away is it?'

The Doctor knew that her concern for Ian had brought her close to breaking-point. 'Gently, my dear. We'll find Ian, I promise you.'

Susan, too, was beginning to panic. 'Suppose the man just goes off with the matchbox?'

Courage, my dear, 'said the Doctor soothingly. 'I know this is all a bit of a nightmare. We've just got to get Ian back and then re-enter the ship.'

'Then will you be able to get us back to our right size?'

'I can certainly try; after all, there's always a chance. But the first thing we've got to do is to find poor Chesterton.' The Doctor looked round. 'Now, this way I think!'

Indomitable as ever, he led them away.

A dark-blue Cadillac, being driven far too fast, hurtled along the narrow country lanes. Swinging round a corner, it narrowly missed PC Bert Rowse, the local policeman, who was proceeding on his leisurely way by bicycle. Bert wobbled furiously across the road, ending up in a muddy ditch.

By the time he'd disentangled himself from his mount and got to his feet, the big blue car had disappeared into the distance.

Farrow opened his briefcase and took out a note-book. He leafed through its contents for a moment, then closed it, shaking his head. The results were absolutely clear, the conclusions unshakeable. He was confident that the results of his unofficial field-test would confirm his theories.

It was going to be a difficult interview. Forester had been polite enough on the telephone, but his reputation as a hard-driving business-man was formidable. But there was a core of steel inside Farrow's plump, fussy exterior. He knew his duty, and he would do it, however unpleasant it might be.

Farrow glanced at his watch. He had arrived early as was his habit. There was just time for a quick cigarette.

He picked up the packet from the ground, took out a cigarette and put it in his mouth. Dropping the packet, he picked up a box of matches, pushing it open with his thumb. He was about to take out a match, when he noticed a ginger cat sunning itself on the doorstep.

Farrow liked cats. He had one of his own. 'Puss!' he called. 'Come on, puss, puss, puss!'

The cat gave him a brief glance of unblinking contempt, licked a paw and started washing its face. Farrow smiled. One of the things he liked about cats was their independence.

A hand appeared over his shoulder, holding the flame of an expensive gold lighter to the unlit cigarette between his lips. 'I see you're a cat lover,' said a deep authoritative voice. Farrow glanced up, accepting the offered light with a nod of thanks and putting the still-open matchbox back on the ground. Mark Forester was standing over him.

Farrow recognized him at once from the frequent newspaper pictures. Dark-haired, thick-set and beetle-browed, Forester wasn't a big man, but somehow he gave off a feeling of power. Standing there in his expensive Savile Row suit, heavy jaw thrust forward, he looked every inch the tycoon.

Farrow struggled to his feet. 'Mr Forester, isn't it? We spoke on the telephone.'

Forester gave him a bone-crushing handshake and a friendly smile. 'I got here as soon as I could.' Typically, Forester came straight to the point. 'I hope you haven't taken any action yet?'

Farrow shook his head. 'Not yet, but I have written my report.' He nodded towards his briefcase.

There was something almost threatening in Forester's deep tones. 'You do realize what's at stake here, Mr Farrow? The early experiments were encouraged by the Ministry, welcomed in fact. I've already geared up my factories, and prepared a very expensive advertising campaign. Everything's ready to start pushing DN6.'

'I'm sorry about that,' said Farrow, not sounding sorry at all. 'Nevertheless, I can't give you the approval you want – and need – to start manufacturing.'

Forester gave him a long, considered look, as if trying to determine the strength of his opposition. 'We could, of course, prolong the experiments, spend more time on the refinements.'

Farrow looked despairingly at him. Didn't the man understand plain English? 'I'm afraid there's much more to it than that, as I've already tried to tell you on the telephone.'

Still Forester persisted. 'If you want to bring in another expert, go over the tests again . . .'

Farrow looked at him almost in pity. 'You're not a scientist, are you, Mr Forester?'

Now it was Forester who pitied Farrow. He bought and sold scientists, just as he'd bought Professor Smithers, the inventor of DN6. 'No, I'm not a scientist.'

Farrow sank wearily into the garden chair. It was a warm day and he felt hot and stuffy in his formal clothes. Soon he would be on his boat in old flannels and an open-necked shirt, feeling the cool breeze from the water – if he could ever get away from this extraordinarily obstinate businessman.

He tried again. 'Let me put it this way. On the surface, DN6 appears to have all the characteristics of a major scientific breakthrough in the manufacture of insecticides. Oh, I can quite understand why you pinned all your hopes on it, particularly as my own Minister was so enthusiastic . . .'

Forester looked sharply at him. Did the old fool know the truth? Did he know the extent to which the future of Forester's vast but shaky financial empire was dependent on the success of DN6? 'Go on.'

'The very exhaustive tests that I have made show that DN6 is *totally* destructive.'

'I thought that was the idea. Smithers tells me it will even prevent locusts from breeding, get rid of them altogether. Think what a boon that would be.'

Farrow's Civil Service veneer was beginning to crack, showing signs of irritation. 'I don't think I'm making myself clear,' he said, which meant, in Whitehall terms, You're being very stupid. With an effort he got a grip on himself. 'There are many insects which make a vital contribution to agriculture, and these insects must not be destroyed. Did you know that?'

'Yes of course.'

'Well, Mr Forester, your DN6 does not discriminate. Quite simply, DN6 is a destroyer. It kills everything it touches.'

5

Death in a Country Garden

Forester stood very still for a moment, for the first time aware of the strange deathly hush all around him. His mind was still trying to take in the size of the problem. 'Is Smithers aware of this?'

Farrow sighed. He had found it difficult to get through to Smithers as well. In this case it wasn't that the man couldn't understand, he simply didn't want to face the truth.

Feeling oppressed by the massive bulk of Forester looming over him, he got to his feet. 'I've tried to express my concerns to Professor Smithers, but he's so engrossed in his discovery that I shall have to break the hard facts to him very gently.'

Concern for Smithers and his feelings was the

last thing on Forester's mind. 'Mr Farrow, are you aware that I shall be ruined if DN6 doesn't go into production almost immediately?'

'That is most unfortunate,' said Farrow primly, 'but you should have waited until we'd given you the go-ahead.'

Forester frowned. 'That's all very well, but it doesn't help me now, does it?' He looked thoughtfully at Farrow, taking in the well-pressed but shiny suit, the worn shoes and the well-brushed Homburg hat: the badge of the medium-grade civil servant. Farrow would be getting a reasonably good salary; didn't he run some kind of little boat? But he was a long way from being rich in Forester's terms.

Moving closer, Forester said confidentially: 'Surely we can work something out? There's a fortune to be made out of this . . .'

Farrow stepped back in horror. 'I don't think I want to go on with this conversation. I shouldn't be seeing you at all, but when we spoke on the phone, you persuaded me to come down here and explain the facts to you in person, and as I was coming down here on holiday . . .'

Forester looked thoughtfully at Farrow. Despite Forester's apparent calm, his brain was in overdrive. Persuasion was out, bribery was out, which left only one option. But Forester had known that all along: that was why he had come prepared. 'What happens now?'

Farrow picked up his hat. 'Well, my holiday officially started yesterday. I've a small boat in the harbour and I'm planning a tour of the rivers of France, I shall telephone my ministry before I go and then post my report.'

Forester made his final attempt. 'Couldn't you leave all that until you get back from your holiday; give me a little time to sort things out?'

'You must know that I can't do that, Mr Forester.'

Forester moved menacingly towards him. 'Do you know why I'm a success, Mr Farrow? Because I've never allowed the word *can't* to exist where my affairs are concerned. There's always a way – *always!*'

'Not this time,' said Farrow flatly. 'This isn't business, it's science. The formula is unacceptable and I can't – and I do mean *can't*, Mr Forester – allow DN6 to go into production.'

Farrow stooped to pick up his briefcase. 'Now I must go and make that phone call.' He turned away.

'Just a moment,' said Forester.

The menace in his tone made Farrow swing round. Forester was covering him with a gun. It was some kind of automatic, Farrow noted, black and quite small. But his mind couldn't really take it in: this sort of thing simply wasn't part of real life.

There was a sharp, flat crack.

Farrow was still refusing to believe what was happening to him when he died, a bullet through his heart.

* * *

With the heavy fluttering of failing wings, a huge furry striped shape dropped from the skies, narrowly missing the Doctor and his two companions. They jumped back, and saw with astonishment the motionless body of an enormous bumble-bee.

'Dear me,' said the Doctor mildly, and moved forward to take a closer look.

Susan cried out in alarm. 'Don't touch it!'

'I think it's dead.'

'It could still sting,' said Barbara.

The Doctor contemplated the striped bulk with detached scientific interest. 'What an awe-inspiring sight!' He turned to Susan and Barbara. 'Now, what chance would human beings our size have, I wonder, in a world of creatures like this bee?'

Susan shuddered. 'None at all!'

The Doctor moved over to the body. 'Let's take a closer look.'

'I haven't taken my eyes off it, grandfather,' said Susan, 'and it hasn't even trembled. I think you're right: it's dead.'

The Doctor bent over the body for a moment, then straightened up. 'There's a strange sort of aroma.'

Barbara nodded eagerly. 'Yes, I've noticed it on all the other dead things.'

'Well, I suppose that is what's killing them,' said Susan.

The Doctor sniffed suspiciously. 'I wonder

what it is that can kill everything in nature like this . . .'

'That's what's worrying me,' said Susan. 'All the different things it's killing: things that fly in the air, things that move along the ground, things that move under the ground. It's all so – indiscriminate.'

Barbara had a more immediate concern. 'Doctor, whatever it is that's killing all these things, could it kill us too?'

'Well, we shall just have to assume that it can,' said the Doctor calmly. 'So, we must eat and drink nothing until we've found Ian and returned to the TARDIS. Now, come along . . .' He broke off, as a dull roar reverberated through the canyon.

Susan cocked her head to listen as the echoes died away. 'What was that? Not thunder, surely?'

'It sounded more like an ancient cannon,' said the Doctor. 'Come along!'

He led them in the direction of the sound . . .

The body of Farrow lay stretched out on the patio. There was a partly-open matchbox close to his outflung hand.

Suddenly, Ian's head appeared over the edge of the matchbox tray. He began struggling painfully out of the box.

The Doctor and his companions toiled along the seemingly endless canyons.

'Well, we're progressing nicely,' said the Doctor encouragingly.

Barbara wondered how he could tell: they had very little idea where they were going. 'I've seen a lot more dead ants, Doctor.'

'Yes, they seem to be rather widespread,' agreed the Doctor.

Barbara shuddered. 'I wonder what would have happened to us if any of those creatures had still been alive?'

'Yes I wonder,' said the Doctor. He seemed quite interested in the idea.

They went on their way.

Ian dropped down from the matchbox and stood looking around him. Directly ahead loomed an enormous round pink shape. It was on such a huge scale that it took Ian some time to realize that it was the face of a man: a dead man.

He turned and hurried away.

Attracted by the flicker of movement, the dozing cat rose, stretched lazily and padded silently after him . . .

Ian turned a corner and ran straight into the Doctor and the others.

Immediately there was a babble of greetings and explanations, as Ian struggled to explain what he had seen.

'A dead man?' asked Susan nervously.

'Yes, he's over here. Come on, I'll show you.'

'Oh please, not any further,' begged Barbara.

'It's taken us ages to get this far. Can't we just go back to the TARDIS?'

Suddenly the Doctor sniffed. 'What's that smell? Gunpowder? Cordite?'

'Yes, of course!' said Ian excitedly. 'From a gun-shot. That would explain the explosion, and the dead man. It's not far. Come on, Doctor, I'll show you!'

Ian and the Doctor set off, Barbara and Susan followed with considerably less enthusiasm.

Soon, all three of them were staring up at the dead man's giant face. Ian pointed upwards to a round hole in the centre of the vast expanse of white shirt-front. 'You see? He's been shot dead.'

'Nothing but death all around us,' said Barbara. 'It's horrible!'

Susan turned to the Doctor. 'What's happening here?'

'We covered quite a lot of ground while we were looking for you, Chesterton,' said the Doctor, 'and every insect we came across was dead.'

'I believe you, Doctor. Susan and I found these dead ants . . .'

The Doctor sat down on top of the matchbox. 'Dead creatures everywhere – and we still don't know what killed them. Now there's this poor fellow: shot – murdered.'

Barbara frowned. 'But who or what would kill all the insects in a garden? I mean, I can understand people wanting to get rid of pests, but surely it must be wrong to kill bees, worms and things?'

The Doctor rose from his matchbox seat. 'Yes, both are vital to the growth of things. We must leave all these mysteries, however, and get back to the TARDIS.' The Doctor sighed. 'Tragic as it is, it's also fortunate for us that everything *is* dead. Creatures our size would be easy prey . . .'

A shadow fell over them.

Susan noticed it first. She looked up and screamed. 'Grandfather!' The others turned and looked up.

Looming over them, green eyes glowing balefully, was an enormous cat . . .

6

Getting Away with Murder

The cat was a terrifying sight, like a tiger as big as an elephant, thought Susan. The glowing green eyes seemed to have an almost hypnotic effect, and she felt a strange urge to run not away from but towards the cat.

'Don't move, any of you,' said Ian in a low voice.

'And don't, whatever you do, look at the cat's eyes,' warned the Doctor. 'Close your own if you have to.'

Susan managed to wrench her gaze away, and screwed her eyes tightly shut.

The cat padded along by the motionless body. The man didn't move or speak this time. It looked at the motionless group of little creatures. They were the same size as mice or birds, but they didn't move and they didn't smell right. Bored, the cat turned away.

'I think it's losing interest, Doctor,' said Ian.

'Maybe so, my boy, but don't relax yet, any of you. One sweep of that paw could smash us to pieces.'

They watched the cat disappear round the side of the building.

'It's gone,' said Ian, and Susan opened her eyes with a sigh of relief.

'Well, we can't move back to the TARDIS just yet,' said the Doctor, 'You know how quickly cats can move, and we could be mistaken for mice. I don't fancy being part of a cat's diet: it might upset my digestion!'

'I suppose it's sort of a protection, though,' said Ian.

Susan stared at him. 'That thing, protection? From what?'

Ian pointed upwards. 'Birds!'

Barbara shuddered. 'This is getting more horrifying every minute.'

Susan turned to the Doctor. 'Can't we make contact with the humans here?'

'No, I'm afraid not.'

'But why not, grandfather? Maybe they could help us in some way.'

'Believe me, it's out of the question, Susan. How could we possibly communicate with them?'

Ian tried to explain. 'Imagine playing a record at the wrong speed, Susan. Our voices would be a little squeak, and theirs would sound like a low growl.'

'Anyway,' said Barbara, 'even if we could communicate, what would they do to us? We'd be freaks. They'd put us in a little glass case and examine us through a magnifying glass.'

'There's an even more important objection,' said the Doctor solemnly. 'The people who live in this house are murderers – or one of them is, at the very least. We can't expect understanding or sympathy from an insane or a criminal mind.'

'Yes, of course, the dead man,' said Barbara. 'Oughtn't we do something about him, Doctor?'

'Ethically speaking, that's a very interesting question, my dear. Responsibility isn't diminished with size, I agree, but surely the real question is this: *can* we do anything? Normally, I wouldn't hesitate: the destruction of the life-force is a frightful thing. But you see how it is? As we are, we're helpless.'

Ian was looking all around them. 'I can't see any sign of that cat anywhere.'

The Doctor drew himself up. 'Then we shall proceed. Our route lies this way, I think.'

A shadow suddenly fell over them, there was a thunderous crunching sound, and the ground shook.

'Someone's coming!' yelled Ian. 'Quick, everybody, hide!'

The little group scattered. The Doctor and Susan took cover at the edge of a flower bed that ran along the cottage wall, but Ian and Barbara ran the other way, and found themselves trapped in the open. The briefcase loomed over them, and the gap under its flap looked like the mouth of a cave.

'Into the briefcase,' shouted Ian. 'It's our only chance.'

The two tiny figures disappeared in to the darkness.

Susan and the Doctor popped up from their hiding place.

'Are Ian and Susan all right?' asked Susan worriedly. 'They nearly got stepped on by an enormous shoe.'

'I rather think they took shelter inside the briefcase. I wish they had come this way with us.'

'Shall we go and look for them?'

'No, Susan, it's too dangerous at the moment.' The Doctor indicated a drain-pipe running down the side of the cottage. 'We'll move over to that pipe.'

Forester calmly looked down at the body of the man he had killed. Beside him was a sharp-faced little man in a white lab coat. His name was Smithers, and he was by far the most agitated of the two.

'You're sure he's dead?'

There was no emotion in Forester's voice. 'Yes, I'm quite sure. I checked.'

'And you say he had a gun?'

'He simply pulled it out of his pocket. He was

trying to blackmail me out of the profits of your formula.'

'Then what happened?'

Forester shrugged. 'I struggled with him . . . somehow the gun must have turned into his body. It went off.'

Smithers knelt and examined the body. After a moment, he rose to his feet. 'I wouldn't try to tell that story to the police if I were you.'

'And why not?'

'Do you think I'm a fool? He's been shot through the heart from several feet away. There are no powder burns round the bullet hole.'

Forester looked hard at him. 'You seem very detached about it.'

'What did you expect: hysterics? I've seen more dead men than you can imagine, Forester. People are starving to death all over the world. Why do you think I turned to agricultural research?' As a young man, Smithers had worked on famine relief projects for the United Nations. He had seen hundreds die while the food that might have saved them was devoured by swarms of locusts, and the terrible sights of death by starvation were burned into his memory.

Smithers looked up at the calm, massive figure towering over him. 'What surprises me is how cool *you* are!'

Forester looked down at the huddled body. 'I don't feel guilty, if that's what you mean. I'm too busy working out the implications.'

'Like the destruction of a whole year's work?'

said Smithers bitterly. 'And if that sounds callous, then let it. Farrow was pushed on me by the ministry. He was a nuisance and a fool, checking every minor detail. I've worked fifteen to sixteen hours a day on this experiment . . .'

Smithers' voice rose in near-hysteria. Forester said soothingly: 'Yes, yes, I know how hard you've worked.'

'You? You don't know anything. All you care about is how much money you can make.' Smithers stared down at the huddled body as if it were an experiment that had gone wrong. 'Why did you have to kill him? Couldn't you have bribed him, bought him off . . . Oh, what's the use . . .'

There was something almost hypnotic in Forester's deep commanding voice. 'Now listen to me, Smithers. I know how much you've put into this project. This doesn't have to mean the end of everything.'

'Of course it does; you've ruined everything. It's all finished, my work wasted.'

'Not necessarily,' said Forester in that same calm, reasonable voice. 'Farrow was officially on holiday. He has a boat, moored in the harbour here, and was going to cross over to France in it – by himself. Now, if the police found a wrecked boat, and the body vanished at sea somewhere . . .'

Smithers looked down at the body, then back up at Forester. 'But how . . .'

'You can leave it all to me. I'll take Farrow's

boat out to sea, wreck the boat and get rid of the body. I can tow a dinghy with an outboard and come back in that.'

Smithers turned away. 'That's your business – I don't want to know anything about it.'

Which meant, thought Forester, that Smithers would go along with his plan. He hated the thought of relying on someone so weak and unbalanced, but there was no alternative – for now.

He made a final attempt to ensure Smithers' co-operation. 'You say all I want out of this project is money, but you want something too, don't you? You want to see the project succeed, to become known as the inventor of DN6.' He paused. 'Well, don't forget you can say goodbye to all that if the truth comes out about Farrow.'

Smithers swung round, his eyes blazing fanatically. 'This project must go through. It's too important to fail. I don't matter, you don't matter . . .' He looked down at Farrow's body. 'And he doesn't matter either, not when we can produce something that will save millions of people from dying of starvation. *That's* what I care about, Forester, and it's all I care about.'

Forester studied him for a moment, then nodded. 'Then just remember: Farrow paid us a brief visit, congratulated you on your success with DN6, and left for his boat.' He picked up Farrow's briefcase. 'I'll just put this in the lab.'

Forester marched into the laboratory, laid the

briefcase flat on its side on the lab bench, and then strode away.

A moment later, two battered, shaken figures emerged from under the briefcase flap.

Ian turned to help Barbara out. 'Let's get out of this thing before someone moves it again.'

They both sat down. Barbara was rubbing her ankle. 'That was worse than a ride on the Big Dipper.'

'Of course, it would have to happen to us,' said Ian resignedly. 'Trust me to pick a movable hiding place.'

Barbara looked round. 'Where do you think we are?'

'Well, we're somewhere inside for a start, and the Doctor and Susan are still outside. How's that ankle?'

'Oh it's nothing really. It got a bang from a big piece of metal.' She laughed. 'Do you know what it was? A paper clip! The whole thing's so ridiculous.'

'Are you sure it's all right?'

'Well, if you could find some water, I wouldn't mind bathing it for a bit.'

Ian jumped up. 'I'll take a look around.'

Smithers was staring broodingly down at the body. He looked up as Forester rejoined him. 'I still don't understand why you had to kill him.'

'I told you, he was trying to blackmail me. He threatened to stop the project unless I promised him most of the profits.'

'Couldn't you have bargained with him?'

Forester shook his head. 'He was asking too much. Remember, he had the power to cancel everything for which we've worked. He threatened to tell the ministry that DN6 was dangerous.'

'But all it does is kill harmful insects. I kept telling him that.'

'Well, now you know why he pretended to be so doubtful all the time. He was preparing the ground for his little scheme.'

Smithers still wasn't satisfied. 'He must have known that I could always have run the tests for another ministry inspector.

'An appeal could have taken weeks, months maybe, to set up. By that time I'd have had to lay off hundreds of workers, close factories, hold up the sales campaign and cancel the advertising. I'd have been ruined. No, he had us over a barrel – at least, he thought he did.'

Dismissing the subject, Forester leaned over the body. 'We'd better put him in the storeroom for the moment. Come on, give me a hand.'

They began to carry the body away.

7

Dangerous Rescue

The Doctor and Susan were hiding behind the concrete ridge that bordered the drain at the side of the house. To them, of course, the ridge was quite a sizeable wall.

Shading his eyes, the Doctor peered across the now empty patio. 'They appear to have gone; the briefcase has gone too.'

'One of them picked it up and took it into the cottage, grandfather.'

'You're sure of that?'

'I popped up and looked when we were hiding.'

The Doctor stood lost in thought. Then he turned and walked across one of the metal struts that formed the protective grille over the drain.

Susan looked on in alarm. 'Don't fall down there, grandfather.'

The Doctor reached the curved opening of the drain-pipe, which looked like the entrance to a tunnel. He stuck his head inside and sniffed. 'Chemicals! I think this pipe goes into some kind of laboratory. Now, suppose that laboratory is the place where the briefcase was taken?'

'Suppose it isn't?'

'We'd still be inside the cottage, my child. And the laboratory is as good a place as anywhere to start looking for Ian and Barbara.'

Defeated by the Doctor's logic, Susan nodded. 'You're surely not thinking of climbing up the inside of that drain-pipe are you?'

The Doctor beamed. 'As a matter of fact, I am. There's simply no other way. Look, the inside is corroded; there are plenty of hand and footholds. With any luck, that chemical smell means it's germ-free as well.'

'But it's much too far for you to climb, grandfather.'

'If it is, I shall have to give up,' said the Doctor placidly. 'But I'm certainly not going to give up before I've tried it! Just think how Ian and Barbara must be feeling, Susan. There they are, only an inch high, with us their only hope of rescue.'

Susan could see that the Doctor was in one of his determined moods. It was pointless trying to argue with him.

'All right, grandfather, we'll try it. But let me go first.' She walked carefully along the metal strut, and the Doctor helped her to climb into the pipe.

* * *

Ian returned from his exploration empty-handed. 'Nothing that way except something that looks like an enormous gas-tap. No water, though, Barbara. Sorry.'

Barbara stood up. 'It's all right, my ankle feels much better now. Let's see what's in the other direction.'

Clinging to a corrugated ridge high inside the drain-pipe, Susan called: 'Are you all right, grandfather? Do you need any help.'

Booming hollowly, the Doctor's voice floated up to her. 'No thank you, my dear, I'm managing very well. Onwards and upwards, Susan!'

Wondering, not for the first time, at the old man's indomitable spirit, Susan resumed her climb.

Barbara and Ian were moving past an enormous rack of giant test-tubes, which loomed above them like some great monument. Further on they came across more puzzling sights: a pile of roundish objects in a huge glass dish, with beyond them a low square block made of something pink.

Ian went to examine the strange pink block, while Barbara moved over to the glass dish.

It held a little pile of spheres, all about the size and shape of a rugby ball, They were greyish-white in colour with a roughly-textured surface.

Barbara examined them curiously. Not eggs, she thought. I know, seeds! Wheat or barley, something like that. She picked up one to examine it, and found it was coated with a slimy, toffee-like substance. She hastily dropped it back in the dish and turned away.

'Look at these things, Ian,' she called. 'They're seeds, aren't they?'

Ian looked across. 'What? Mmm, yes, wheat I should think. You come and look at this.'

Barbara moved over to him, rubbing her sticky fingers. 'Lend me your handkerchief, will you Ian?'

Still absorbed in the block, Ian passed her the neatly-folded display handkerchief from his breast-pocket. 'Do you know what this thing is, Barbara? It's a book of litmus papers.' He sighed reminiscently, recalling his days as a science master. 'The times I've stood at a lab bench with a piece of litmus paper in my hand! Makes a handy seat, anyway.'

Ian sat down and Barbara sat beside him, furtively wiping her fingers on his handkerchief.

He made a sweeping gesture. 'You know what all this is, Barbara? Some sort of laboratory. That explains all the dead insects we saw: there's some sort of pest-control experiment going on. Just makes it more dangerous for us, of course.'

'What do you mean?'

'While we're this size, what can kill insects might very well kill us too.'

'The Doctor said something about not eating or drinking anything,' said Barbara slowly. 'I'd forgotten.' Hiding her hands behind her, she rubbed her fingers with the handkerchief.

'Better be careful about touching things as well.' Ian jumped up and went to look at the seeds. 'Look, these things are coated with something. They must be working on a new insecticide and they've sprayed these samples with it.'

Barbara came over to him. 'Couldn't it be some kind of preserving oil?' she asked hopefully.

'Well, maybe, but I doubt it.' He sniffed. 'It's got a weird smell . . . I'd keep well away from it.'

Barbara considered telling him that his good advice had come far too late, but then what was the use? It would only worry him, and there was nothing he could do. She wondered how long before the poison would start to affect her. Or perhaps it was harmless to humans after all.

'Ian, listen, we've got to find the others and get back to the TARDIS.'

'I know, but I can't seem to work out how. We're so high up here, it's like being trapped on a mountain. Have you got any bright ideas?'

Barbara shook her head. 'I only wish I had.'

There was such despair in her voice that Ian looked at her in concern. 'Look, we *can* get down, you know. All we need is a ball of string!'

Barbara tried to enter into the spirit of things. 'String would be too thick. What we really need is a reel of cotton – oh, it's all too ridiculous!'

'We've got to forget how absurd things are and concentrate on the main problem, all right?'

Barbara managed a smile. 'All right.'

'What about the briefcase, Barbara? There's all sorts of stuff in there. If we could find enough paper clips we could link them up and make a metal ladder.'

'It's certainly an idea.' Barbara's tone made it clear she didn't think it was a very good one.

Ian was hurt. 'Well, it's worth a try. Come on, Barbara, don't give up.'

'I am not giving up. I'm perfectly willing to try anything, you know that.'

Ian started moving back towards the briefcase. 'We'll have to get it open somehow. I don't fancy working in the dark . . .'

'Maybe there's something in the briefcase that will tell us what this insecticide stuff is . . .'

Ian looked at her in surprise. 'Well, maybe. Does it matter? Getting away from here is what counts.'

He set off and Barbara followed him, still rubbing her fingers with the handkerchief. Somehow the stuff just wouldn't seem to come off.

The Doctor clung to a niche in the pipe, hearts pounding and lungs straining for breath.

Susan's voice echoed down from above. 'Are you all right, grandfather? It's not far now, I can see light up above.'

The Doctor braced himself for a final effort. 'Coming, my child, coming!'

Wearily he resumed his climb.

Ian was sitting on a brass plate, heaving at a brass turret – the catch of the briefcase.

‘It doesn’t move downwards, that’s for sure,’ he grunted.

Barbara stared up at him. ‘Try left to right.’

‘Great minds think alike,’ called Ian. He shifted position and heaved again. ‘No, that’s no good either, I’ll try right to left.’

‘All right,’ called Barbara. ‘Good luck!’

She stood looking up at the struggling figure on the briefcase, quite unaware of the giant shape hovering above her. Then she heard a strange rustling sound and turned . . .

At his final attempt, Ian felt the briefcase catch give way. He heaved again, there was a loud click, and the briefcase flap flew open. ‘Hurray, success! I’ve done it, Barbara!’ There was no reply. Ian looked down. ‘Barbara, are you . . .’

Barbara was standing perfectly still, staring straight ahead of her. Crouched before her was the terrifying shape of an enormous fly.

8

Whirlpool

The huge fly scrutinized Barbara with its many-faceted eyes as if unsure what to make of her. Its body quivered, its huge translucent wings vibrated gently, and it was rubbing its front legs together, producing an eerie rustling sound.

Barbara opened her mouth to scream for help, but no words would come. Watching helplessly from above, Ian saw her body crumple and slump to the ground. The fly moved nearer, as if it were curious. What would happen, thought Ian, if it decided she was dead – didn't flies feed on the dead?

Suddenly there was a thunderous crash and the room seemed to vibrate. The fly took off with a whirring of wings, hovered for a moment, and then settled on the little pile of treated seeds.

Jumping down from his perch, Ian picked up Barbara's unconscious body and carried her into hiding behind the briefcase.

Smithers came into the room and began taking rags and cleaning spirit from a cupboard under the lab bench. He was irritably aware of Forester, who was standing in the doorway watching him. Smithers looked up. 'You don't have to watch everything I do, you know.'

Forester stayed infuriatingly calm. 'I just like to know what's going on.'

'Well, here's something you don't know. There's a patch of blood on the patio flagstones. You don't seem to have noticed it.'

'Can you get it out?'

Smithers waved a battered can. 'This ought to shift it.'

'I won't forget this, Smithers.'

'Oh yes you will. You'll forget all about it, once it's over. Shooting Farrow, disposing of the body – you'll rub it right out of your mind.'

Forester smiled. 'Well, of course, once it's over.'

'You needn't think I'm doing this for you, either, Forester. It's for the project. If there's one chance in a million of making it work, then I've got to take it.'

'Quite so,' said Forester. 'It's simply a question of the greater good.'

'Your greater good, you mean. You've committed murder and now it's got to be covered up.'

'We're only being sensible, Smithers. Practical.'

'Oh yes,' sneered Smithers. 'It was practical all right, making me an accessory.'

Forester raised his eyebrows. 'Making you?'

'Yes, making. You knew perfectly well how I feel about the DN6 project, how much work I've put into it, what it means to me. That's why you took me out and showed me Farrow's body, wasn't it?'

Tired of Smithers and his ranting, Forester shrugged. 'Yes, of course.'

Smithers looked at him with something very like hatred. 'You'd do anything to get what you want, wouldn't you?'

Forester's voice hardened. 'Wouldn't you? *Aren't you?*

Smithers glared at him for a moment. Then he dropped his eyes and went off to clean up Farrow's blood. Forester followed close behind him.

The Doctor was lying beside a huge round metal-bordered hole, divided into segments by struts radiating from a smaller central circle. All around him was a gleaming metal plain, bounded on four sides by smooth high metal walls. He was lying beside the plug-hole in a stainless-steel laboratory sink.

Susan knelt beside him, bathing his face with some of the water that occasionally splashed down in giant drops from the tap above. 'Wake up, grandfather! We did it. We climbed all the way to the top.'

'I know, my dear child, I know,' said the Doctor wearily. 'The smell of those chemicals must have overpowered me for a moment. Just let me rest for a while.'

'I think there were people talking in the room just now: I could hear a low rumbling noise. They seem to have gone now.'

The Doctor sat up. 'Our own voices sound rather odd. Do you know, I think this metal sink is acting as a sort of echo chamber.'

'We ought to try to find the others, grandfather. Do you think there's a chance they might be here?'

The Doctor looked at her eager face. 'I don't know, my child. I simply don't know.'

Barbara recovered consciousness with a start, pulling away from Ian's supporting arm.

'Easy now,' he said reassuringly.

She stared blankly at him. 'Ian?' Suddenly she clutched his arm. 'Did you see it?'

'The fly?' Ian nodded. 'Two men came into the room and frightened it away.'

Barbara shuddered. 'I just turned round and there it was. Its whole body was quivering – and those eyes . . .'

'Well, it's over now. The fly is dead.'

Barbara stared at him. 'How do you know? You said it just flew away.'

'It did, but it landed on those seeds. It seemed to die almost instantly.'

'Are you sure?'

Ian gave her a puzzled look. 'Certain. I saw it when we were hiding just now.'

Barbara got up. 'I want to have a look.'

'Are you sure? Do you really want to?'

'Yes, I do. It's all right, Ian, I'm over it now.'

He reluctantly led her over to the dish of seeds. The dead fly was sprawled across them.

'Look,' said Ian. 'You can see the insecticide still glistening on its legs. Must be pretty lethal stuff: the fly died within seconds after touching it.'

'Oh, stop it, can't you?'

Ian stared at her in astonishment. 'Barbara?'

With an effort she got herself under control. 'Ian, there's something I've got to . . .'

A distant voice interrupted her. 'Barbara . . . Ian? Can you hear me?'

'It's Susan!' said Ian delightedly.

The voice came again. 'Can you hear me, either of you?'

Barbara pointed. 'It seems to be coming from over there. Let's go and look for her.'

She moved away, but Ian put a hand on her arm. 'What were you going to tell me?'

'It's all right, it doesn't matter now. Don't you see, Ian, if Susan's found a way in, that means there's a way out for us. We can get back to the TARDIS!'

'Yes, of course. Come on, let's look for Susan.'

In the metal sink, the Doctor was saying: 'Even if they reply, you won't necessarily hear their voices, you know. This sink is acting as a sound box, increasing the volume of your voice.'

'How far will my voice carry?'

'I've no idea, my child.'

'Are the people who live here liable to hear me shouting?'

'No, no, Susan. Our voices are much too high for them. It's a different frequency altogether. Mind you, a dog might be able to hear us. Why don't you try again?'

At the top of her voice, Susan yelled: 'Ian! Barbara!'

Her voice boomed hollowly around the metal sink and this time there was a reply.

'Susan, Doctor! We're up here!' shouted Ian from the edge of the sink.

'Hallo up there!' called Susan delightedly. 'It's them, grandfather. It's really them!'

Up on the edge of the sink, Barbara said: 'Did they really climb all the way up that sink pipe?'

Ian grinned delightedly. 'They must have done. The thing is, can we all get down again?'

They heard Susan calling up to them. 'Come down to us. You can climb down the plug chain.'

'All right,' yelled Ian. He looked at Barbara. 'I reckon it must be about thirty feet on our scale. Can you manage.'

'I'll manage,' said Barbara determinedly. 'It's worth any effort to see those two again.'

Ian smiled, as delighted as she was. 'I know. Come on, then. I'll go first.'

The plug chain looked to Ian and Barbara like the anchor chain of an ocean liner, and the massive links gave plenty of foothold. Ian carefully started to make his way down . . .

'Ian's started,' said the Doctor. 'The sooner we're all out of here the better.'

'Will we be able to get down the pipe safely, grandfather? It was bad enough coming up.'

'It should be easier if anything. And remember, it's our one sure way back to the garden – and the TARDIS.'

Susan looked up. 'Barbara's starting now.' Barbara cautiously followed Ian on to the giant chain. His voice floated up to her. 'How are you doing?'

'Not too badly. There seems to be plenty to hold on to.' She carefully felt for another link with her foot.

Aware all the time of Forester's ironic gaze, Smithers scrubbed the last of the blood from the flagstones, threw a handful of earth over the clean patch, and ground it in with his foot. 'I want to get this muck off my hands. I'll use the sink in the lab.'

Forester nodded, and followed him in to the cottage.

In the sink, the Doctor and Susan heard the

reverberating crashes that signalled the arrival of normal-sized humans.

'They're coming back,' said the Doctor worriedly. 'Someone's coming into the laboratory!'

On the chain, Ian and Barbara heard the sound as well. 'Somebody's coming,' yelled Ian 'Go back up, Barbara. Don't wait for me – hurry!'

For Susan and the Doctor, there was only one place to hide. 'Back down the pipe, Susan,' said the Doctor. 'Hurry now.'

Susan lowered herself through the plug-hole.

Smithers stood at the laboratory bench, looking at the dead fly in the dish of seeds. 'Look at this! The fly must have died the instant it landed.'

Forester looked casually at the seeds. 'Part of the batch you sprayed with DN6.'

'Think what this stuff will do to locusts. With DN6 we can wipe them out.'

'You don't have to keep on persuading me,' said Forester wearily. 'I've read every report on every test you ever made.'

Smithers frowned. 'You know, I still don't see how Farrow hoped to get away with lying about DN6. He must have known we'd make a complaint.'

'Oh, don't keep on about it,' snarled Forester. 'All right, so he was a fool to think he could get away with it. He thought he had us over a barrel.'

'You said he'd written a faked report, condemning DN6?'

'Yes, it's in his briefcase.' Forester went to the briefcase and fished about inside, quite unaware of the two tiny figures cowering beneath the case. He produced a ring-backed notebook, looked at it for a moment and then tossed it on the desk, where it fell open. He took a wad of loose papers from the briefcase. 'There are some draft notes here . . . don't want them . . .'

Shoving back the papers, Forester continued rummaging through the case. After a moment he took out an unsealed envelope containing a thick wad of typed papers. He took out the papers and glanced through them. 'Here we are! We must get this off to his head of department right away, with a few slight amendments of course.'

Smithers seemed to lose interest. 'I don't want to know about that. I don't want to listen.' He put in the plug and began running water into the sink.

Ian peered out from his and Barbara's hiding place. 'That was a near thing.'

'What's happening?' whispered Barbara.

'One of them seems to be standing at the sink . . .' A hollow, rushing, drumming sound filled the air. 'He's turned on the tap – and the Doctor and Susan are still in that sink!'

Smithers scrubbed his hands, shook off the excess water, and pulled out the plug. Forester threw him a hand-towel, and he started drying his hands.

Smithers tossed the towel on to the lab bench, and both men left the laboratory.

In the basin of the laboratory sink, swirling water formed a whirlpool around the plug-hole, and rushed away down the pipe . . .

9

Suspicion

Ian cautiously emerged from his hiding place. 'I'm getting used to interpreting those weird noises now. That last crash must have been the door closing.'

'You're sure they've gone?'

'I'm not sure about anything.'

They looked at each other for a moment, trying not to think about the tragedy that had just occurred.

Barbara spoke first. 'The Doctor and Susan . . . they must have been drowned.'

'We don't know that . . .'

'Then we must find out.'

Ian nodded wearily. 'Yes, of course. I'll go down.'

'I'm coming too.'

'Are you sure? You can stay here if you like.'

'I said I'm coming with you, Ian!'

Barbara was almost shouting, and Ian looked at her in concern. 'Are you all right?'

Barbara was far from all right. Her head was aching, and she was beginning to feel dizzy. This latest tragedy was almost more than she could bear. But she managed to say quietly. 'Yes, I'm all right. You go first.'

Ian went over to the edge of the sink, clambered on to the massive chain, and began climbing down. Barbara cautiously followed.

It wasn't too difficult a climb, and they reached the bottom without any problems. The bottom of the sink was scattered with water droplets like tiny ponds.

There was no sign of the Doctor and Susan.

Ian went over to the plug-hole, stretched out flat and peered down it.

Barbara came over to him. 'See anything?'

Ian got up, shaking his head. 'It's too dark. I'm afraid there's no hope.' It was a terrible end, he thought, for someone who had once roamed through space and time – flushed down a sink like some unlucky bug.

Barbara looked hopelessly at him. 'What are we going to do, Ian? what can we do, like this?'

Ian shook his head. He had no comfort to offer for once.

A hand appeared over the edge of the plughole. It was followed by an arm, and then by the rest of Susan. She gave them a cheeky grin, then turned and shouted down the plug-hole. 'They're here, grandfather. I told you they'd be all right!' She helped the Doctor to heave himself out of the plug-hole after her.

Ian gaped at them. 'I don't believe it! I just don't believe it!'

Barbara was equally amazed. 'Doctor . . . Susan . . . but how . . .'

'We hid in the overflow trap, just below the plug-hole,' explained Susan. 'The water rushed past us, like a huge waterfall. It's a good job there wasn't any more or the overflow would have filled as well.'

The Doctor finished brushing himself down and beamed at them, quite unaffected by his adventure. 'You see, my friends, you can't get rid of us as easily as that!'

The living room of the cottage had been converted into a simple office, and here Forester was busy at the typewriter, adjusting the late Farrow's report. He turned the report into one of unqualified praise for DN6 simply by reversing the dead man's conclusions.

The last page, the one with Farrow's signature, fortunately read: 'I very much hope that the minister will accept my conclusions, and feel able to act on them immediately.' It made the perfect ending for the altered report.

Forester arranged the papers, and put them into an envelope addressed to the minister.

'There we are, the report's ready. I'll send it off today.'

Smithers was slumped in an armchair, staring broodingly in to space. 'Yes, all right.'

'There's just one more thing,' said Forester thoughtfully.

'What?'

'Farrow's head of department was expecting a call from him.'

Forester reached for the telephone.

Smithers jumped out of his chair. 'You can't do that, you'll give everything away! They'll know it's not him speaking.'

Forester smiled, enjoying his own audacity. 'Just you leave this side of things to me.' He picked up the telephone.

The telephone system at the cottage was antiquated even for its time. There was no direct dialling: all calls had to go through the local telephone exchange, which was contacted simply be lifting the receiver.

The local exchange was part of the village shop, which also happened to be the village police station. The exchange was in the cluttered storeroom behind the shop. It was run by Mrs Rowse, with occasional assistance from her husband, PC Bert Rowse, the village constable.

Hilda Rowse was a thin, energetic, inquisitive woman who took a pride in knowing everything about everybody for miles around. She had long been curious about the old cottage. After standing empty for many years it had been bought by a mysterious London company, which had promptly moved in vast quantities of scientific equipment. The cottage was now inhabited by a strange little man called Smithers, who kept lights burning all night, never seemed to go out, and had all his supplies sent down from London.

When her switchboard indicated a call from the cottage, Hilda plugged in and lifted her earphones, all her senses alert. 'Hallo, exchange operator,' she said brightly.

Forester gave a Whitehall number and waited for the call to go through.

'How do you know who to speak to?' asked Smithers anxiously.

'Don't worry, I've been dealing with these people for years.' He took a handkerchief from his pocket, stretched a section of it tautly over the mouthpiece and spoke into the phone. 'Oh hallo, is Mr Whitmore there please? Arnold Farrow speaking. Sorry about the bad line . . . I'm fine, thank you. Yes, I'll hold on.'

Covering the mouthpiece with his hand, Forester turned to Smithers. 'You see? The secretary asked how I was. I told you it would be all right.'

Hilda looked up as her husband Bert came into the room, buttoning his spare police tunic. He had come home to change, and he was still grumbling about his experience with the blue car. 'If I ever find who was driving that thing . . .'

Hilda interrupted him. 'Something funny's going on.'

'What sort of funny?'

'There's a call from the old cottage: bloke says he's Mr Farrow. You know, that nice fussy little bloke who came in about provisions for his boat.'

'So?'

'Well, it doesn't sound a bit like him, that's all.' She listened on her headphones. 'The line's gone all muffled now as well – and it was all right when he first put through the call.'

Forester was talking into the mouthpiece, doing his best to imitate Farrow's fussy, precise delivery, and relying on the handkerchief stretched over the receiver to disguise his voice.

'Yes, Mr Whitmore, I'll send in a report today. The tests are all satisfactory, most satisfactory. Yes, it's a terrible line, isn't it . . . I'd say DN6 shows about sixty per cent improvement over most insecticides. What? No, I know I'm not usually so enthusiastic, but this is something extraordinary . . . Yes, I'm crossing over to France tonight . . . No, I don't mind losing the day. My boat's moored close to here, and the night passage is a lot more peaceful . . . Yes, I'll take care. Right, I'll send in the report then. You'll issue the necessary authorizations? Good, I'll tell Mr Forester, he'll be delighted. Goodbye.'

Forester put down the telephone and sat back triumphantly, stuffing his handkerchief back into his pocket, 'Perfect! We'll get the go-ahead as soon as he gets the report. Things couldn't have gone better.

Smithers could scarcely believe his ears. 'Then – there's a chance we're going to get away with it?'

Forester smiled. 'I don't see what can possibly stop us!' But he was reckoning without the curiosity of Hilda Rowse, not to mention the ingenuity of the Doctor and his companions.

10

The Doctor's Plan

The Doctor and his companions were standing grouped around the open notebook, which looked like a sort of low platform, marked out for some mysterious game.

'It certainly wasn't here before,' said Ian. 'I think it must have come out of the briefcase.

Susan looked down. The sheer size of the writing on the paper made it difficult for her mind to make sense of it. 'It's part drawings, part letters and figures. I think it must be some kind of formula.'

Barbara studied the giant symbols. 'Do you think it could be the formula for the insecticide, Doctor? If it is, it'll tell us what we're up against. You might even find a cure.'

'What do we need a cure for? asked Ian. 'If

we're going to do anything we've got to stop it being produced.'

Susan nodded. 'That's right. We need a cure only if someone got poisoned by the stuff.'

'Yes, all *right*,' snapped Barbara.

The Doctor looked curiously at her for a moment. 'Well, I suggest we take a closer look at this oversized document. The more we know about our enemy the better.'

Ian pointed. 'Those things over there are definitely molecular structures, Doctor.'

'You may well be right, Chesterton. I wish we could get an overall picture of the whole thing.

'Could we lever it up somehow, and stand away from it?' suggested Barbara.

Susan laughed. 'It would be like looking at a giant advertising poster!'

'I'm afraid we'd never move it,' said Ian. 'It's much too heavy.'

'Lend me your notebook, will you Susan?' said the Doctor suddenly.

Susan produced a notebook from the pocket of her overalls and handed it over.

The Doctor took a silver pencil from his pocket. 'Now what we must do is make a kind of map of this thing, reducing the scale. Now, each of you mark out a section with your feet, then, as I come to you, call out the things you see written beneath you.'

Peculiar as it was, the Doctor's scheme seemed to work, and in a surprisingly short time Susan's notebook held a scaled-down replica of what was on the giant page.

The Doctor studied it. 'This is the formula for the insecticide, right enough.' He handed the notebook to Ian. 'It's a bit rough, but it tells the story.'

'I'm a bit rusty on all this, Doctor. What's this – phosphoric acid?

'That's right, my boy. And this indicates the amount of organic esters.'

'Then this must be mineral nitrate . . .' Ian handed back the notebook. 'That's about as far as I go.'

The Doctor looked round the little group. 'This is a formula for a particularly efficient insecticide, with just one vital difference. The inventor has come up with an insecticide that is ever-lasting. In time it will seep through the soil, and get into the drinking water.'

Barbara looked anxiously at him. 'How will it affect human beings, Doctor?'

'Absorbed in sufficient quantity, the insecticide could kill human beings too.'

'You mean if they were to eat and drink a lot of contaminated food and water?'

'Even if they come into contact with it, Barbara. The insecticide is capable of penetrating the skin to get into the bloodstream.'

'Then why do we just go on sitting here?' shouted Barbara. 'Why don't we do something to . . .'

'Gently, my dear, gently,' interrupted the Doctor.

'I'm sorry, I . . .' She broke off, her head in her hands.

Susan put an arm round Barbara's shoulders. 'Are you feeling alright?'

'A bit giddy, that's all. I think I must be hungry.'

The Doctor held up a warning hand. 'That's another point to remember. We'd better not eat – even if we could find any food in this place.'

'The less we talk about food and drink the better I'll like it,' said Ian grimly.

The Doctor rubbed his chin. 'The water in the tap is probably safe. I want to go over in that direction anyway. I spotted something nearby which might well provide a solution to this business – a telephone. Come along, all of you, and I'll explain my plan.'

The Doctor and Ian stood staring up at the towering black bulk of the old-fashioned telephone.

They had all paid a refreshing visit to the sink where they had been able to drink some water from a conveniently still-dripping tap. As Susan pointed out, when a drop came down whoever it hit got not only a drink but a refreshing face-wash as well. Now they were ready to attempt to carry out the Doctor's plan, which was quite simply to communicate with the outside world by means of the telephone.

If they could only get out some kind of message about a dangerous formula and a murdered man, they could surely spark off an investigation. Luckily for them, the telephone in the lab had been rigged up as an afterthought and there were tangled loops of wire coiled about the base.

'Well it's climbable,' said Ian.

The Doctor nodded. 'No doubt, but how heavy is that receiver?'

Susan approached, carrying a cork the size of a small drum. 'We've found the very thing. We can use these to prop up the receiver. There are lots more over there.' She pointed to Barbara, who was approaching, very slowly, with another cork.

Ian went to meet her. 'Are you sure you're all right. You don't look too good.'

'I keep telling you, Ian, I'm fine. It's just that I haven't eaten for ages, that's all it is. Don't make a fuss!'

Ian turned to the others. 'Susan and I will do the climbing. You pass the corks up to Susan, Doctor, and she'll pass them up to me.'

The first part of the plan worked well enough. Ian climbed right up to the long thin ledge underneath the receiver; Susan climbed half-way up, and the Doctor passed the cork to Susan, who passed it to Ian.

The Doctor went back to Barbara, who had put down her cork and was sitting hunched up on it.

'You look very tired, my dear.'

'I'm afraid I am a bit, Doctor.'

'Well, you rest, we can manage alright now. But I'll need your seat, I'm afraid.'

Barbara nodded wearily and sat down on the floor.

The Doctor carried the cork to the telephone and passed it up to Susan, who passed it to Ian.

'Right,' called Ian, 'you'd better all come up here now.'

Susan and the Doctor struggled up to join him on the ledge.

Ian had already placed the two corks in position. There was one at each end of the platform, at the places where they would be inserted when, or if, the receiver could be lifted.

'Can we do it with just three of us?' asked the Doctor as he climbed on to the platform. 'I don't think Barbara is well enough to help.'

'It's all right, I'm here,' gasped Barbara. Ian and Susan helped her on to the ledge.

Ian led them to the left-hand cork. 'Now, Susan, we're all going to try to lift this end of the receiver. When we've go it high enough, you push the cork underneath it.'

He lifted the cork into place, so that all Susan would have to do was shove it forward. Susan raised her hands to the cork.

'Ready!'

Ian turned to the others. 'Come on, then.'

The Doctor, Ian and Barbara got their hands under the receiver and began to heave. It seemed to weigh a ton, but slowly, slowly it lifted, and at last it was high enough for Susan to thrust the cork underneath.

'Got it!' she said triumphantly.

The three lifters stood gasping for breath for a moment, then moved to the other end of the receiver.

'Right,' said Ian. 'Same thing this end!'

Again they heaved and strained, lifting the heavy receiver upwards. At last it was high enough, and Susan thrust the second cork into the gap. 'We did it!'

A buzzing came from the switchboard in the telephone exchange, interrupting Bert Rowse, who was absorbed in police paperwork. 'Hilda,' he yelled, 'Come and answer this thing, it's driving me crazy.'

Hilda bustled forward, her curiosity aroused. 'It's the old cottage again.' She put on her headphones and plugged in. 'Hallo! Exchange here. What number do you want?'

At the other end of the telephone, the Doctor, Ian and Susan were grouped underneath the raised mouthpiece of the handset, yelling with all their might.

'*Can you hear us? Put us through to police!*'

Barbara was waiting at the listening end.

'Any good, Barbara?' called Ian.

'Nothing . . . not a thing . . .' Barbara slumped to a sitting position on the ledge. She was really dizzy now, and the telephone seemed to be swinging round like a fairground ride.

Ian was too caught up in their enterprize to notice. 'We can't have failed, not after getting this far.'

The Doctor sighed, 'I'm afraid we have, and it's all my fault. I thought it was worth trying.'

'Let's try once more,' said Ian determinedly.

'I don't think it'll do any good, Ian,' said Susan wearily.

'We must try. I'll go and warn Barbara.'

Ian turned and saw for the first time that Barbara was sitting huddled up and shaking on the ledge.

He went over to her. 'Hey, you've been overdoing it.'

Her voice was weak. 'Yes, maybe I have.'

'I'll go and get you some water, that'll make you feel better.'

He saw that Barbara was twisting his handkerchief in her hands. He tried to take it from her, but she snatched it away. 'What are you doing?'

'I just want my handkerchief for a moment. I'll soak it in water for you.'

'No! Don't touch it,' she muttered feverishly. 'You can't have it . . .'

Seeing something was badly wrong, the Doctor and Susan hurried along the ledge.

Barbara stared wildly up at them. 'Don't let anyone touch . . . handkerchief . . .' She slumped over sideways unconscious, the handkerchief falling from her hand.

11

Barbara's Peril

The Doctor knelt to examine Barbara for a moment. He put a hand on her forehead, and then checked the pulse in her neck. He took out his pencil and picked up the handkerchief, sniffing it carefully.

He looked sternly at Ian. 'When you were away from us, you didn't eat or drink anything?'

'Definitely not.'

'Then she must have touched the insecticide.'

'I didn't see her do it – and she didn't say anything. She *was* acting a bit strangely earlier on though . . . she borrowed my handkerchief.'

'Where were you, at that time?'

'Over by the pile of seeds, I think.' Ian looked worriedly at the Doctor. 'The ones that had been treated with insecticide . . .'

The Doctor spread his hands. 'It's obvious enough what happened. Barbara got some insecticide on her hands, probably from the seeds, and borrowed your handkerchief to try to get it off.'

Susan knelt beside Barbara and stroked her forehead. 'Why didn't she tell us?'

Suddenly Barbara's eyelids fluttered and she opened her eyes. 'What happened?'

'It's all right, Barbara,' said Susan. 'You fainted, that's all.'

Barbara saw the handkerchief on the end of the Doctor's pencil and realized her secret was out. 'That insecticide . . . That's why I feel like this, isn't it Doctor?'

The Doctor tossed the handkerchief away. 'Yes, my dear. You got some of it on your hands, didn't you? It was very wrong of you not to tell us.'

Barbara stared up at him. 'Doctor, am I going to . . .'

'No, no, my dear. I'm sure this attack you've just experienced is only temporary. It will soon pass.'

While Susan went on caring for Barbara, the Doctor drew Ian aside. 'It's urgent that we get Barbara back to normal size, Chesterton. At the moment her protective cells can't cope with the poison in her bloodstream. That dose of insecticide will become seventy times smaller – and seventy times less dangerous – if we can get her back to full size.'

'You're sure of this, Doctor?'

'Certain, my boy. We've just got to get her back to the ship.'

'Then what are we waiting for?' Ian turned back to Barbara. 'How are you feeling?'

'A bit ropy, I'm afraid . . . If I could only have some water.'

'We'll get you some. Then we're going to take you back to the ship. You'll be better there.'

'Just give me a moment, Ian.'

Ian looked worriedly at her, remembering the Doctor's words. 'Quick as you can then, Barbara. We've got a long journey ahead of us.' He looked worriedly at the Doctor. 'You *can* get us all back to full size, can't you Doctor?'

'Of course I can, dear boy.'

Reassured, Ian turned back to Barbara.

'Of course I can,' said the Doctor again. Then, to himself, he quietly added: 'I hope.'

Hilda Rowse took a boiled sweet and sucked it thoughtfully. 'I don't care what you say, there's something odd going on there.'

Bert looked up from his paperwork. 'Where?'

'The old cottage.'

'Look, Hilda, I've got all these reports to initial and the foot and mouth circulars to get out . . .'

'First they're impersonating people, now they've left the phone off the hook.'

'Ring 'em up then.'

'How can I, when the receiver's off?'

'I don't know, I'm a copper not a telephone operator. Buzz them or something.'

Hilda thought for a moment. 'I'll put on the tone, then.' She reached for a key on her switchboard.

'Tone' is a loud and annoying high-pitched whine, intended to inform people that they've left their telephone off the hook and irritate them into doing something about it. To the Doctor and his companions, still perched on the telephone, it was a deafening howl.

Susan clapped her hands over her ears. 'It's going right through my head!'

'This is awful,' yelled Ian. 'The quicker we get down the better. I'll lead the way.'

'What?' screamed Barbara.

'I said I'll lead. Susan, you come next – give Barbara a hand. Doctor, you wait until last and help the girls down to me.'

The Doctor, however, had followed Susan's example. 'I can't hear a word you're saying, Chesterton: my hands are over my ears.'

'I said I'm going down first,' shouted Ian.

'All right, all right, no need to bellow,' said the Doctor irritably. 'Now listen, my boy, I think you'd better go down first.'

They started to climb down.

Forester picked up the telephone and immediately got an earful of tone. Snatching the receiver away from his ear he jiggled the crossbar a few times and slammed down the receiver. 'What the devil's wrong with the thing?' He looked across at Smithers who was slumped gloomily in his armchair. 'And come to that, what's the matter with you?'

'Farrow's the matter.'

'Oh, snap out of it, man. All you've got to do is stick to the story, it's simple enough: Farrow was here, he approved DN6, he left for his boat, and as far as we know he's on the way to France.'

'I wasn't thinking about that side of things.'

'Then what's bothering you?'

'You said Farrow tried to blackmail you, threatened to send in a negative report on DN6 unless you cut him in on a big share of the profits.'

Forester lit a cigarette. 'That's right, he did.'

'It doesn't fit,' said Smithers obstinately.

'Doesn't fit what?'

'Farrow's character. He was meticulous when he went over DN6: he queried every test, went over things three or four times. He was infuriating but I'd swear he was honest.'

Forester let out a cloud of smoke. 'You're very naïve, aren't you Smithers?'

'Maybe but I'm not a fool. I can tell an honest man from a crook. It simply wasn't *in* Farrow to come up to you and say "Give me most of the profits or I say DN6 is no good". It doesn't fit.'

'Now you listen to me, Smithers,' said Forester coldly. 'Why don't you stop torturing yourself, stick to the story we've arranged, and everything will be fine.'

'Will it, Forester? Perhaps . . .'

* * *

'It's no use, Ian,' said Barbara. 'I won't go any further.'

'Don't be ridiculous, Barbara.'

They were by the sink area and Barbara, although much refreshed by a drink of water, was refusing to go on.

'Oh, come on, Barbara, please,' begged Susan. 'We're wasting time.'

'No, for the last time, no! I'm not important any more.'

'You're important to us, Barbara!'

'Please, all of you, will you listen?' said Barbara urgently. 'I only got a tiny speck of that stuff on me, but if a normal-sized person got a lot on them, wouldn't they get dizzy, start blacking out, maybe *die*?'

She looked at the Doctor, but he made no reply.

'We all saw what that insecticide did, out there in the garden. What will be the consequences if it's produced and used in quantity? Wouldn't you say it was our duty to stop the destruction of a whole planet, Doctor?'

'Yes, Barbara. I would. But at the moment *you* are our most immediate concern.'

'Our responsibility hasn't altered, Doctor.'

'Barbara, listen,' said Ian desperately. 'The longer we stand here arguing, the greater the hold that poison will get on your system. We're taking you back to the TARDIS and that's final. Don't you understand, you're *ill*. You must let us take you, or you could die.'

Barbara obstinately shook her head.

'Please, Doctor, you make her see some sense.'

Sadly the Doctor shook his head. 'I'm afraid there's nothing I could say, my boy. You see, Barbara's quite right.'

Ian stared unbelievingly at him, then turned away in despair.

Barbara went up to him and put a hand on his shoulder. 'We must find a way to stop this thing, Ian. We *must*!'

12

Plan of Action

PC Rowse looked up from his paperwork as Hilda came marching out of the shop, where she'd been engaged in a lengthy conversation.

'Who was that?'

'Tom.'

Tom was the shop's delivery boy, one of the last survivors of a fast-dying breed. He spent his working day trundling up and down the country lanes on a massive bicycle with a big basket on the front, delivering goods to the local inhabitants.

'He cycled past the old cottage today,' Hilda went on. 'He says there's a big blue American car in the driveway.'

Bert sat up. 'Did he now?'

'Just like the one that nearly ran you over,' said Hilda innocently.

'How do you know? You weren't even there.' PC Rowse rubbed his chin. 'Still, it might be the same. If it is, I wouldn't mind a chat with the driver.'

Hilda looked at the switchboard.

'They still haven't put back their receiver . . .'

Forester jiggled the telephone a few more times, and then slammed it down. 'This is ridiculous, I've got some very important calls to make. Are there any other phones round here?'

Smithers, still slumped and brooding, said dully: 'What? Oh, there's a phone in the lab.'

'Maybe that's where the trouble is. If the phone's off the hook or something . . .'

To Forester's surprise, Smithers got up. 'I'll go and see. I want to have a look at Farrow's draft notes.'

'Why?' demanded Forester.

Smithers walked out of the room without answering him.

Forester took a small black automatic out of his pocket – the gun with which he'd shot Farrow. He checked the gun, put it back in his pocket, and hurried after Smithers.

On the lab bench, the Doctor and his companions were still discussing their next move.

'All right, all right, I agree,' said Ian at last. 'We ought to do something about this insecticide.

But what? While we're this size, we don't even know what's going on.'

'Size doesn't affect intelligence,' said the Doctor severely. 'We are still capable of intelligent speculation.' He took hold of his lapels, in his favourite speech-making pose. 'We know two things for certain. One, the insecticide is dangerous. Two, a man has been murdered. Surely the only logical assumption is that there is a connection between the two. We also know that the murdered man knew the truth about the insecticide – it was in his notebook. Is it not overwhelmingly likely that the the man was murdered to prevent him from revealing that truth?'

'I'm sure you're right, Doctor,' said Ian. 'But what can we do?'

'We can draw attention to this place, my boy. All we need is something like – a fire!' The Doctor rubbed his hands. 'That's it. There's nothing like a good fire!'

Ian regarded him warily. Sometimes he thought the old boy could be dangerously irresponsible.

He turned to Barbara. 'What do you think?'

'Actually, Ian, it's a very good idea. If we could set fire to this place it would bring people here from outside.'

'That's right,' said Susan. 'Then they'd find that poor man's body.'

'Precisely,' said the Doctor. 'Once people start asking questions about what's going on here, our work is done!'

'The gas tap!' said Ian suddenly. 'If we could turn that on . . .'

'What good would that do?'

'I'll show you,' said Ian. A thunderous crashing interrupted him as the doors were flung open.

'Quick, everyone,' shouted Ian. 'Hide! Get well back, behind those test-tubes . . .'

Smithers hurried into the laboratory, then stopped short as he noticed a dark shape huddled on the floor. He bent down to examine it.

Forester came into the laboratory. 'What are you doing?'

'It's the cat – it's dead!'

'Get rid of it then,' said Forester callously. He went over to the telephone, which was still giving out its piercing tone, and immediately saw the corks holding up the receiver. 'Aha!' He removed the corks and the maddening noise cut out.'Smithers! What are these doing under the phone?'

Smithers was still puzzled by the dead cat. 'It's fur seems to be sticky.' He sniffed his hands. 'It's DN6!'

'I want an explanation,' insisted Forester. 'Did you put these things under the phone to stop me using it?'

'No, of course not.'

'Then who did?'

'I don't know and I don't care. Will you listen to me, man? This cat was killed by DN6!'

Smithers jumped up, ran to the tap and rinsed

his hands, then went to the briefcase and tipped its contents out on the desk.

Forester looked at him in astonishment. 'What are you doing now?'

'I want to see Farrow's draft notes.'

He rummaged through the briefcase's contents, tossing aside Farrow's matches and cigarettes, and finally discovered a sheaf of roughly scrawled notes. 'Ah, here they are!'

'What are you trying to prove?' demanded Forester.

'I want to know *why* that cat died of DN6.' He studied the notes for a moment. 'Listen, this is what Farrow says: "I took a sample of DN6 and sprayed a part of the garden. I shall examine the results of the test on my next visit . . ."'

'Look, does all this matter?'

'It matters very much,' said Smithers evenly. 'I don't think these notes were written by a blackmailer.' He headed for the door.

'Where are you going?'

'To discover the results of Farrow's field test!' Smithers marched out.

Forester was just about to follow him when the telephone rang.

13

Fire!

Forester snatched up the receiver. 'Yes?'

The voice at the other end – Hilda's official, posh voice – said: 'I see you have replaced your receiver, Mr Smithers.'

'This isn't Smithers . . . I'm afraid the extension receiver was left off. I'm very sorry.'

'Is that Mr Farrow?'

'Farrow? No, I'm not Farrow either.'

'Is Mr Farrow available? I have a call from London for him.'

'Just a minute, I'll see . . .' Forester felt a sudden surge of panic. The fact that the caller was asking for a dead man, the man he'd killed, gave him an odd sinister sensation. Who could be calling Farrow? His office in Whitehall presumably . . . Would it be better to take the call or not?

In the exchange behind the village shop and post office, Hilda waited eagerly. Bert, her policeman husband, hovered nervously beside her. 'I don't think you ought to be doing this, Hilda.'

Hilda ignored him. To her, the fact that the people at the cottage had replaced their telephone gave her a chance to communicate with them, and to investigate the goings on. Because there were goings on at the cottage, of that Hilda was sure.

Covering the mouthpiece with his handkerchief, Forester said: 'Farrow here . . .'

'You see,' whispered Hilda. 'It's the same man, disguising his voice.'

'Get him to talk a bit more.'

Hilda put on her official voice again. 'I have a London call for you, Mr Farrow. Will you accept the charges?'

Now Forester was really baffled. Who on earth was calling Farrow? Surely his Whitehall office wouldn't reverse the charges? There was only one way to find out. 'Yes, all right, I'll pay for the call.'

'One moment please, I'll put you through . . .' Hilda turned to Bert. 'Well?'

'It's odd, isn't it – they do sound alike.'

'I think you ought to go out there and check, Bert.'

'Maybe. Let's think for a bit.'

Hilda turned back to the switchboard. 'Mr Farrow? I'm sorry, your caller has broken the connection. Perhaps he'll call again. Sorry you've been troubled.'

She pulled out the plug. 'That was one and the same man, Bert, no doubt about it. It wasn't Mr Farrow. And Mr Farrow hasn't been in to pick up his supplies like he said he would.'

'Well, maybe I'll just take a ride over there. There's still that business of the car nearly running me down, I haven't forgotten that.'

He put on his helmet. and Hilda smiled in satisfaction. When Bert put on his helmet, that made things official.

Forester mopped his brow with his handkerchief, and thought for a moment. There was still Smithers to deal with. He hurried out of the laboratory.

Very soon afterwards, an elaborate plan was under way on the lab bench. The Doctor, Susan and Barbara were heaving on the lever that turned on the gas-tap. The tap was the old-fashioned kind, set into the bench, with a nozzle that was meant to take the rubber tube leading to a bunsen-burner.

The lever stretched out horizontally above just

within arm's reach so they were almost swinging on it. Under their joint efforts it started to move.

'It's coming,' said Susan.

'All together now,' gasped the Doctor. 'We just want to loosen it, remember, so it can be turned on quickly.'

They heaved away.

Ian, meanwhile, was struggling to extract an enormous match, bigger than himself, from Farrow's box. He had just managed to wrestle it out of the box when Susan came running up to help him. 'The gas-tap's ready to be turned on now.'

'Good. Now, I've managed to wedge the matchbox against the side of the briefcase. What we've got to do, Susan, is run this against the side of the box.' He nodded to the brown bulbous end of the match.

Susan grinned. 'Rather like using a battering ram.'

Not far away, the Doctor and Barbara were sliding a metal canister marked 'DN6' across the smooth surface of the lab bench.

'All right, I think that will do,' gasped the Doctor. He stepped back to study the canister's position. 'Excellent. That should be directly in the patch of the gas-jet.'

Barbara looked puzzled. 'But surely all we'll do is melt the tin, Doctor.'

The Doctor rubbed his hands. 'I chose this canister with particular care, my dear. I think it must be an experimental prototype. It's pressurised – one of those spray things. Our only problem is going to be getting far enough away from it before it explodes.'

'Explodes?'

'Oh yes, my dear,' said the Doctor happily. 'When this thing goes off it will be, to us, the approximate equivalent of a thousand pound bomb!'

Forester caught up with Smithers in the garden not far from the cottage. He was kneeling in a flower bed, studying the devastation his invention had created. 'It's killed everything . . . everything!

A hated voice called: 'Smithers!'

He turned and saw Forester towering over him.

'I want you to help me get Farrow's body in the boot of my car. We'll take him down to the harbour when it's dark and get him on his boat . . .'

Smithers interrupted him. 'You knew all the time, didn't you? The formula went wrong somehow, so DN6 became too powerful, and almost ever-lasting. Farrow found out.'

'What are you talking about?'

'DN6 kills *everything* Forester: insects, bees – even worms. It killed the cat. It'll poison *people*, if enough of it builds up in their bodies. Farrow told you, didn't he?'

'It doesn't matter now, Smithers. Farrow's dead.'

'But he was right. DN6 is too dangerous to be

used. Farrow was going to put an end to the project. That's why you murdered him.'

'Yes,' said Forester calmly. 'That's why I killed him. He left me no choice when he told me he wouldn't authorize DN6. I had too much money sunk into it. I had to kill him, and now I've started I've got to see it through – all the way. And so must you, Smithers.' He took the little black automatic from his pocket and gestured at Smithers with it. 'So you'd better just co-operate. Come on, back to the laboratory. Move!'

Dazedly, Smithers moved away.

Barbara and the Doctor watched as Ian and Susan, carrying the huge match between them, hurled themselves forward, like two medieval knights charging a castle gate with a battering ram. The end hit the igniting strip on the side of the matchbox and skidded straight off again. Overbalancing, Ian and Susan fell to the ground.

The Doctor clicked his tongue disapprovingly. 'No, no, Chesterton. Try to hit the box at a sharper angle. More vigour, more force!'

Ian wearily picked himself up. Recovering his giant match he waved it at the Doctor. 'Have you ever tried lifting one of these things?'

Still full of enthusiasm, Susan scrambled to her feet. 'Come on Ian, let's have another go!'

Taking hold of the match, they charged again.

This time, perhaps because of the Doctor's good advice, it worked. There was a bright flash and a small explosion; the end of the match burst into flames.

'He's done it,' gasped Barbara. 'Well done!' called the Doctor. 'Come along Barbara, we must turn on the gas.'

They ran to the lever and pulled it the rest of the way down, listening to the fierce hiss of the escaping gas.

'Turn it down a little.' called Ian. 'We don't want to get roasted . . . that's better. Now, you two, get behind the water tap.'

As the Doctor and Barbara took shelter, Ian and Susan edged forward with the blazing match, its heat beating on their faces.

'Here we go, Susan,' said Ian. 'Easy does it.'

They pushed the burning end of the match into the stream of gas. The gas ignited with a roar that sent them staggering back, and a jet of flame leaped out, playing around the metal canister.

Susan and Ian ran to join the Doctor and Barbara in the shelter of the water tap.

Nothing happened for several long moments. Then the side of the canister began glowing cherry-red. The Doctor stood watching the roaring gas-jet with the simple enjoyment of a child at a firework display. He rubbed his hands. 'It can't be long now . . .'

'Keep under cover as much as you can,' warned Ian. There'll be bits of metal flying all over the place if that thing does explode.'

Susan seemed to be enjoying herself almost as much as the Doctor. 'It feels like that time we were in an air raid, doesn't it grandfather? do you remember?

'I remember very well, my child. And what infernal machines the Kaiser's Zeppelins were!'

A distant rumbling filled the air, coming steadily nearer. 'Quiet!' warned Ian. 'Someone's coming.'

The door of the laboratory burst open, and a protesting Smithers was shoved inside at the point of Forester's gun.

'Think what you're doing, Forester,' he pleaded. 'DN6 is potentially more dangerous than nuclear radiation.'

'Get the briefcase,' ordered Forester. 'I want all Farrow's notes destroyed.' Suddenly he saw the blazing gas-jet. 'What's going on? What's that?'

As Forester moved forward for a better look, the canister exploded . . .

14

A Question of Size

Forester staggered back, hands to his face, dropping the gun. Smithers snatched it up and stood there uncertainly, wondering what to do next.

That decision was made for him when a scandalized PC Rowse rushed into the room and snatched the gun from him.

PC Rowse looked down at the still-dazed Forester, who by some miracle seemed to have escaped serious injury. 'He'll live. Now, there are quite a lot of questions that need answering.'

'I've got quite a lot to tell you,' said Smithers. 'But there's something you ought to see first. It's in the storeroom.'

'Turn off that gas tap,' ordered Bert Rowse. 'Do you want to kill the lot of us?'

Smithers went over to the tap and turned it off – the flame had already been blown out by the explosion. He saw a scrap of charred paper, part of the label on the exploded canister. He could just make out 'DN6'. He crumpled the scrap of paper and threw it away.

'Quick, quick!' ordered the Doctor. 'Down the plug-chain everybody. We must get back to the ship. Susan, help Barbara will you?'

To Ian's surprise, the Doctor rushed over to the pile of treated seeds and scooped up one, wrapping it in his cloak.

'Careful with that, Doctor,' warned Ian. 'It's covered with poison.'

'Yes, yes, I know all about that,' said the Doctor tetchily.

'What do you want it for anyway?'

'You'll see, my boy, you'll see. Now, do get a move on, Chesterton.'

They began climbing down the plug-chain after Susan and Barbara.

The journey back down the waste-pipe and across the garden to the TARDIS was long and tiring, but largely uneventful. Now it was over, and Ian was standing by the console, anxiously watching the Doctor as he worked feverishly at the controls. He glanced across at Barbara who lay semi-conscious in a big chair, with Susan at her side.

'How much longer do we have to wait, Doctor? Barbara's very ill now.'

'I'm doing the best I can, Chesterton. First I had to repair the scanner: we might as well be blind without it. Now I simply have to duplicate, in reverse, everything that happened when we landed.'

'Is there anything I can do?'

'That giant seed by Barbara's chair, put it on that little table there where I can see it. Here, use this when you do it.'

The Doctor slipped out of his cloak, and Ian used it to pick up the seed and put it on the side-table. It had been quite a job getting the giant seed back to the TARDIS, but for some reason the Doctor refused to part with it.

The Doctor's hands moved quickly over the controls. 'In about ten seconds we'll be moving into the space-time continuum. Ten . . . nine . . . eight . . . seven . . . six . . . five . . . four . . . three . . . two . . . one!'

The central column began to rise and fall. 'It's working, Chesterton. We're growing, and the ship's growing back to normal size.'

Which was why there was nothing to be seen, thought Ian. With ship and people growing at the same rate there was no change discernible to the eye. Except . . .

Ian followed the Doctor's gaze and saw that the giant seed was growing smaller, smaller, until it seemed to disappear. Ian shook his head. 'That's incredible. The seed just vanished completely.'

'Oh no, I don't think so, Chesterton,' said the Doctor. He went over to the table and picked something up. 'No, the seed hasn't vanished, not quite. Look!'

There in the Doctor's palm was a very ordinary-looking seed.

Ian turned to look at Barbara. She was conscious again, shaking her head ruefully. 'I feel as if I'd been put through a wringer. And I'm so thirsty!'

Susan gave her a glass of water and Barbara drank thirstily. 'I never knew water could taste so good.'

The Doctor came over and patted her head. 'Well, here we are then! The patient is beginning to look her usual self again.'

'Thank you, Doctor,' said Ian quietly.

The Doctor bowed. 'Always at your service, dear boy.'

'What happened in the laboratory?' asked Barbara.' I don't remember much after the explosion.'

'I'm happy to say our plan succeeded,' said the Doctor. 'We didn't manage to set the laboratory on fire, but we did attract attention. Do you know, just as I was about to climb down the chain into the sink I'm pretty sure I saw a policeman come into the room.'

Barbara sighed with relief. 'Thank goodness for that. But what about us? Will we ever get back to our right size again?'

The Doctor held out his hand. 'There's your answer, my dear!'

Susan looked puzzled. 'That's not the giant seed you brought in, grandfather?'

'The very one, my child.'

'Then we really are back to our proper size!' said Barbara delightedly.

'Most certainly we're back.' A groaning sound filled the TARDIS and the central column stopped moving.

The Doctor moved to the console. 'What's more we've arrived, somewhere.' He looked round the weary little group. 'Now, while I set things up and find out where we are, why don't you all go and have a good scrub?'

As his weary companions filed away, the Doctor was already absorbed in checking the instruments.

He switched on the scanner, and found himself gazing at a screen filled with visual static. 'Dear, dear, dear, dear.' said the Doctor crossly. 'Now isn't that irritating. I've just repaired that thing, and now look at it! Oh well, we shall just have to go out and see where we are . . .'

The Doctor stood gazing at the console lost in thought, trying to work out where he was. Still on Earth, he was sure of that. But the time period – data there was a little vague.

He wondered what had happened to the scanner, and what was going to happen next. He would break the news about going out exploring to the others when they came back. It would be a nice little surprise.

The Doctor brightened. The unknown could be terrifying, but it was stimulating and fascinating as well.

Outside in the ruins of London the Daleks were waiting . . .